THE
DARKEST
HOUR

M.J. RYDER

@iamselfpub
www.iamselfpublishing.com

This book is dedicated to all of the strong, inspirational women who have shaped my life and made me the man I am today: Gran (Sheila), Mum (Debbie) and my two wonderful sisters, Nicky and Kate.

PART 1

THE DARK ENVOY

In the cold dark depths of space, an ancient evil stirs from its slumber...

Prologue

"Wake up Varrus, your life is mine."

Varrus slowly swam to consciousness. He opened his eyes to reveal nothing save the impenetrable black of space.

The voice thundered inside his head. *"So, you have come at last. I've been expecting you..."*

Varrus gulped. He could still feel the sharp stab of pain as he had died at the boy's hands. By using magic to evade death, he had made a terrible, terrible mistake.

"Cease your trembling mortal. I am Skargyr and you are mine now – there can be no escape. Worlds have lived and died while I have waited for someone of your qualities to find their way into my cursed prison. You shall know me now as your master."

As memories of his former life slowly returned to him, Varrus regained some of his composure. "I serve no one!" he spat, "I am my own master."

"Foolish mortal – I am your GOD! Bow down and worship me and I shall consider sparing your worthless soul."

Varrus felt his life-blood turning to magma, his body wracked with pain. To question the will of the voice had been a mistake. He had to make the pain stop. He had no other choice. He howled his subservience to the star-god.

From that moment, his fate was sealed. Varrus' voice was barely a whisper: "What would you have me do my Lord?"

"Destroy magic Varrus; bring an end to the threat of men to my plans. Stop their magicians and close their wells of magic so that at last I might be free. Do this my servant, and when the time comes, I might just spare your pitiful soul."

Varrus shuddered as he considered the size of the task before him. Closing the sources of magic would be no simple feat, and even worse still, he knew his nemesis – the boy – would hold the key.

"Boy," Varrus thought to himself ruefully. Such was the nature of time in this strange place, chances were the boy was already a man, and maybe even with child. He shuddered again as he felt the weight of the star-god's gaze upon him.

"Your wish is my command… master."

1

Phae stood wide-eyed and trembling as all around her young apprentices ran for their lives. She searched around desperately for means of escape, but the fire was everywhere. Searing flames leapt across bookshelves and between timber roof supports, stoked by burning texts that exploded like fire-crackers as their magically-imbued pages caught alight and combusted, adding their material to the raging heat of the inferno.

Across the room Master Kulgrim was furiously attempting to organise some of the more experienced magic users into fire-fighting teams to try and quench the blaze. It was no good. One by one their exits were cut off, leaving only a single doorway out into the streets.

Kulgrim called out to her.

"Phae, run! We need to get out of here now!"

Phae flinched as she watched the chaotic scene unfold about her, her hands still ablaze with the fierce fire magic that she had been so desperately trying to control. She couldn't move. Her whole body was paralysed with fear.

Kulgrim called out to her again. "Phae!"

She looked up, and saw him gesturing to the exit that was already starting to crumble as the age-old wooden building slowly burnt to the ground. She watched as above them one of the huge supporting roof beams started to crack. The remaining mages ran for the door, Kulgrim with them. At the last moment he paused and turned back. He ran over to her and scooped her fragile body up in his arms. "Your father would kill me if I left you alone in here."

Just then the cracked roof beam started to give way. The whole building shook as the remaining supports struggled to take the extra weight. Kulgrim dashed for the door, but it was already too late. He stumbled as the beam fell, and Phae was sent crashing to the floor. She turned for sight of the brave water-mage, but the smoke was so thick she could barely see at all.

Somewhere amidst the smoke, a cry of pain reached her ears. The sound of Kulgrim's cries snapped her out of her paralysis. She struggled to her feet. "Master Kulgrim?"

The voice of the water-mage was faint. "Phae…"

"Master Kulgrim, where are you?"

"Down here!"

Cautiously she felt her way through the smoke, following the coughs of her would-be rescuer towards their source. More through luck than judgement, she stumbled across the mage a few feet away, trapped under a pile of wood and debris.

Phae knelt down and tried to move him, but realised her hands were still ablaze with magic. She struggled for control, but amidst the noise and confusion of the fire, she was helpless. Tears streamed from her eyes.

She did her best to brush them away on her sleeve. "We need to get you out of here."

"Can't," the mage coughed. "Too hot… legs broken. Tell your father I'm sorry…"

As the water-mage started to fade, Phae could feel her frustration continue to grow. The flames on her hands doubled in size as all around her the fire burned even more brightly, and the heat grew even more intense. She wanted it to stop.

She looked around desperately for some means of moving the injured mage, but couldn't see anything of use amidst the smoke. She never meant to hurt anyone. She never meant to…

Phae fell to her knees as the flames finally closed in around them, sucking away the final few gasps of air left in the Halls. It was hopeless.

"I don't want to die," Phae wept. On the floor beside her, Kulgrim lay perfectly still. If he hadn't passed already, it wouldn't be long now. "It's all my fault…"

"It's not your fault Phae – you're not going to die."

"Father?"

A funnel of air pierced the smoke above her, pushing the choking fumes away. There were strong magics building around her. The flames that had just moments before threatened to consume her suddenly started to retreat. As the smoke cleared further she could just make out the floating form of her father, arms outstretched, extending his magics across the ravaged Halls, slowly beating back the flames until they were finally reduced to nothing.

As the flames died, Phae dared a glance at the stricken water-mage by her side. Though his breathing was faint, he was alive; but only just. Breathing seemed a small mercy for poor Master Kulgrim when every breath he took was torture. Phae knew he didn't have long.

As the fire dissipated, small teams of mages bravely re-entered what was left of the Halls to quench the smouldering remains. As they did so, the still distant figure of her father descended from his position up in the rafters to land amidst the charred ruins of his once-proud Halls. Phae struggled to her feet and ran over to him. He held her tightly in his arms until the flames that covered her hands faded and she was restored to her normal self. That the returning mages had seen the shameful mark of her crime was in no doubt. She buried her face deeply in her father's cloak.

"It's alright Phae, it's over now. The fire's out and everyone is safe."

Phae looked up into her father's eyes. "Everyone?"

Her father shot a concerned look over to a group of mages struggled with a laden stretcher. Even from this distance he could tell the experienced Master Kulgrim had only a slim chance of survival at best. He looked down at his frightened daughter whose eyes streamed with tears. Beneath his arms he could feel her fragile form trembling. He wiped her tears away as best he could. "*Everyone,*" he said firmly.

She struggled to free herself from his grasp. "You're lying!" she cried. Several mages turned their heads towards them.

"Phae I'm not lying to you."

"Yes, you are!" she replied. "Can't you see that his life-force is spent? He'll be dead within the hour and it's all my fault!" Wiping her tears on the back of her sleeve, Phae ran from the Halls. Her father called out and was about to run after her when all of a sudden he stopped in his tracks. The weight of two dozen pairs of eyes fixed on him, waiting for his instruction. They had seen everything. They knew what had caused the fire in the Halls. They *knew* who was responsible. He surveyed the scene before him. The Halls of Meditation were lost. The walls were nearly all burnt to the ground, and only the husk of the building's skeleton remained, its charred, blackened frame a sharp reminder of the vastly dangerous, uncontrollable power his daughter wielded.

Callum sighed as he considered his options. There was nothing else for it – the Halls of Meditation would have to come down.

* * *

The night was dark; far darker than it had been for many months now. Even the great pole star *Illustus* shone dimly, and the old world's moons were but two faded smudges in an overcast canvas of grey. As the night drew on, a cold easterly breeze swept across the island, bringing with it a rolling bank of dense fog that settled on the city streets and enveloped the Magical Isle in a cold, damp, impenetrable mist.

Even from his position high atop the tallest tower of the Wizards' Citadel, Callum could only faintly make out the shapes of a few towers and rooftops tall enough to pierce the fog. Not even the street-lanterns of the wizards could penetrate the mist; their bright lights reduced to nothing more than faint, eerie glows as the greatest city in the realm of men was reduced to nothing more than a panorama of dull grey.

Callum pulled his cloak tightly around him as the cold easterly wind bit into his skin, bringing with it another rolling bank of fog to shroud the streets in mist. It was a cold night already, but he knew they were not over the worst of it yet. Strange that such weather should hit them in the middle of the summer months, but a welcome relief from the cloying intensity of the hottest summer days anyone could remember for at least half a century.

He looked to the east in search of even the faintest rays of light that might signal the approaching dawn, but found the horizon as chocked with thick cloud and mist as were the city streets below him. At best guess, he didn't have too much longer to wait. He had already spent most of the night pacing atop the tower, waiting for the coming day. A few more hours wouldn't hurt. At least it would give him time to think.

It was at times like these that he missed Kiera most. She had been gone nearly six months now, and if the absence of her mother was having a significant effect on their daughter Phae, the absence of his wife was really starting to take its toll. Even after all their years of marriage, he loved her just as much now as he did the day he had first set eyes on her, in a small tavern in the town of Osten.

He thought fondly of the time he and his best friend Aaron had first encountered the young swordswoman. She had saved them from a local gang of thugs that day, and from that moment on their fate together had been sealed. Their path had taken them to the forbidden lands in the south, and then further south still as they found themselves embroiled in the midst of a dark conspiracy to bring the realm to its knees. Kiera's own personal journey had culminated in her taking the path of the Lintari, and so joining a small band of mysterious warrior-folk bound to the earth and gifted with its powers that they might act as defenders of the old world and keepers of the peace.

Of course, they had met many other companions on their travels, and none more important than the water-mage Lena, whose keen intelligence and bravery had saved Callum's life more times than he could count. While she had always been a powerful, if unrefined magic-user, she had grown in stature while travelling with Callum and his company, and had grown to a power far in advance of any water-mage he had ever met. She quite literally shared a "bond" with the ocean, that was at once both fiercely impressive yet terrifying for anyone who knew as he did, the great power a mage of her kind could draw from the sea.

While there were few mages more powerful than Lena, there were certainly none he trusted more, and she had grown, along with Aaron and Kiera, to be one of his closest and dearest friends. Of course, while he himself had fallen helplessly in love with Kiera as their adventures took their course, this wasn't to say that he was the only one to fall in love. While they had travelled, Lena had grown ever closer to his friend Aaron, and now, some years later, the two lived in a small house on the edge of the city.

Callum supressed a laugh as he imagined what Aaron would think of him now, standing alone atop the Citadel, looking out over the mist-shrouded city, waiting for the new dawn. If he wasn't complaining about the weather, or his insatiable hunger, Aaron frequently spent much of his time trying his very best to rile Kiera, or find some excuse to pick on Callum. Now he thought about it, Callum was certain if his friend knew what he was doing at this moment, he'd probably tell him to stop moping and get some sleep. Yes, that was Aaron alright – blunt, sarcastic, but in his own strange way, incredibly caring and thoughtful.

Callum paused for a moment and considered going to find his friend for a chat and an early morning cup of tea. Though Aaron would no-doubt complain bitterly at having his sleep disturbed, Callum knew he wouldn't mean it really. Aaron would more than willingly give his life for him, and he'd likewise do the same for his friend. They'd been through too much together not to know what the other would think.

He sighed as his thoughts worked their natural way back to the main reason he couldn't sleep; the reason he stood atop the 'Isle's highest tower in the middle of the night. Phae was at once his deepest, most profound love, yet also the source of his greatest problems. She had only just recently celebrated her fifteenth birthday, and yet from the moment she had come forth into the world, she had been trouble.

The problem came of course, from her parentage. Born of a union never before witnessed in the realm of men, Phae had blood inside her with the potential to make her one of the most powerful beings the old world had ever known. Both he and Kiera had studied hard before finally agreeing to have children, and though he'd always wanted some of his own, the prospect of melding mage with Lintari had at first been one he was not keen to consider. "The danger is just too great," he had said – the Lintari didn't have children for a reason, and for Kiera to have a child with the most powerful magic-user in the realm was asking for trouble.

They just hadn't realised how much.

Callum sighed fondly as he considered his daughter in all her flawed brilliance. For all the difficulties she had caused since her birth – all the fires, the earthquakes, and even the odd creature summoned from beyond, he wouldn't change her for the world. From the moment she had been born a bond had been formed between them far stronger than any he could have ever imagined. It wasn't just a bond of parenthood – it was a bond of magic.

Kiera couldn't quite understand when he had tried to explain it to her, but there was something between them – something they shared – that made them far closer than mere father and daughter. He couldn't quite put his finger on it, but it was there nonetheless, always in the background; an awareness of the other closer still than even his bond with his wife. What was it old Kulgrim had said? "Magic works in strange ways," yes that was it, and certainly no stranger than it had worked to help bring about Phae – a child of unparalleled magical potential, but a child nonetheless. She was growing up fast, and while even her formative years had proved troublesome, her journey into adolescence had taken her problems to a whole new level, and every day Callum could see she seemed to be in less control. The fire in the Halls of Meditation would be only the beginning.

He had to do something, but he didn't know what.

Phae was a danger: both to herself and to the people around her. Were she not his daughter, Callum knew that the citizens of the Magical Isle would be far less "forgiving" of her episodes. Only last week she had unleashed a mini-tornado in the library...

Callum sighed again as he considered his options. Though the day would remain cold well into the morning, the first rays of dawn were at long last starting to break their way through the mist on the horizon.

It was time to make a decision. It was time to see Aaron.

2

In her bedroom, Phae paced restlessly.

She couldn't sleep. Truth be told, she hadn't been sleeping well for over a week now as her body changed and she sought to control the raging fire that grew within her.

This night though, this night was different.

Though she hadn't heard the news directly, she *knew* that poor Master Kulgrim had died in the night, just as she predicted he would – the first victim of her frightening power. She had wept bitterly when she felt his passing from the mortal plain, though by now her tears had long dried up. Now all she felt was anger: anger at herself; anger at her parents; anger at her mother for not being there; anger at her *life*. Why couldn't she just be *normal*?

Phae sighed as she paced her way across her cluttered bed chamber, working her way carefully around the piles of books and trinkets that she had thrown from her desk in an earlier moment of despair. She glanced across the room. In the far corner sat her pack. Ever since her first "accident" she had kept it half-packed and ready… just in case.

Needless to say, she had never *meant* to leave really – she loved her parents too much for that. The act of packing and making to escape had been cathartic, a plan she never *intended* to see through.

But now was a different matter. Someone had died. She couldn't stay on the 'Isle any more.

She stared long and hard at her backpack that lay slumped in the corner. Her mother had bought it for her on one of the rare occasions she had returned home in the last two years. She said it would be just right for the summer when she promised she would take her to Lake Forever – one of the wonders of the realm.

"Like that will ever happen," Phae thought to herself sullenly. Too many times her mother had returned home only to leave almost as soon as she had come; called away by the mysterious pull of her order that kept her away from the 'Isle, often for many months at a time.

Of course, her father had taken her camping on the mainland whenever he had the chance, but compared to the tales of adventure she had so often heard from Aaron (whose story-telling was second to none), camping with her father in the woods surrounding Pegwell paled in comparison.

Ever since she had learnt about the fantastic beauty of the Lake it had been a place she had always wanted to visit, a place she hoped she might find some comfort and peace. Legend had it that the strange magical properties of the Lake even offered healing to the sick and those in need. If ever there was a person in need at this time, it was her. She hoped desperately that the Lake might offer her some release from her torment – even if just for a few days – before she returned to the 'Isle and the comfort of her parents whose forgiveness she worried she might never earn. She would certainly never forgive herself for the terrible accident that had led to Master Kulgrim's untimely death. He didn't deserve to die: she did.

Phae strode decisively now over to her pack and picked it up to test its weight. It sure was heavy, and she hadn't even filled it with food yet.

She brought it back over to her bed and emptied its contents on her quilt to see if there was anything she could conceivably leave behind. She looked at the maps she had found and at once threw most of them on the floor. She didn't intend on going any further than the Lake and for that she would need just the one.

Along with the maps she discarded her compass, her small collection of pretty stones, her favourite blanket, and the framed picture of her parents given to her on her birthday. As it fell to the floor the glass protecting the artist's drawing smashed, sending hundreds of tiny shards across the floor to bury themselves in the thick carpet pile. Phae winced as she reached over to pick the small picture out of its discarded frame. She folded it up and put it in her breast pocket. Some things were just too precious to throw away.

Hastily stuffing the remaining items into her pack, Phae picked it up again to check its weight. It was better now, but still by no means perfect. Along with the food she had stored in a cupboard down the hall, it would still be a burden for one of her stature, but it was a burden she would have to endure. With her pack now securely fastened and pulled high upon her back she risked a quick glance out of the window, picked up an extra jacket from her pile of discarded clothes, and made her way to the door.

Outside, in the long, daunting corridors of the east wing, the Citadel was silent. If she stretched out her senses far enough she could just make out the sound of the night-watch patrolling the floor below; their faint hollow footsteps the only sound of movement she could detect.

She turned back briefly as she made the first tentative steps of her escape. A tiny voice in the back of her head beckoned her back inside. Phae shook her head vigorously and dismissed the thought at once. She had given up on her planned escape at least half a dozen times or more in the past. She would not give up again.

All of a sudden Phae's body was wracked in pain. Memories flooded her mind. Somewhere in her head the voice of poor Master Kulgrim called out to her telling her to pass on a message to her father. She did the best she could to ignore it but just then the pain increased further still. She winced and brought her hand to her head. Her whole body shook. As she trembled she could feel her pack slipping from her shoulders.

Just then, a sound reached her from down the hallway. Members of the night-watch were climbing the stairs. Even at this distance she could hear their muffled voices getting closer. She covered her face in her hands. As the footsteps drew nearer, piercing beams of light shone down the corridor and swept side to side in search of intruders. Phae could see two mages approaching, and recognised the man on the left as one of her father's friends. He certainly wouldn't be happy if he learnt she had tried to run away again...

Phae removed her hands from her eyes.

Removed her hands from her eyes.

She stared down at her hands and realised with mute horror that her hands simply weren't there. She looked down to her feet to find nothing there – her entire body had vanished. She was invisible!

Phae held her breath tightly as the two watchmen spotted her pack lying on the floor and hurried over to pick it up. One of them – the one she didn't recognise – tutted and shook his head sadly. "Miss Phae must be planning another one of her little adventures I see."

His companion nodded agreement. "That or she's trying to run away again," he said softly. "Can't say I blame her really."

"Poor girl," the first man sighed. "So much power, and so young too. Master Callum's certainly going to have to find something to do with her. She can't go on as she is anymore. Not now. Not now Kulgrim's passed."

The second man picked up the pack and examined its contents. "She's trying to run away alright," he said. "Look there's a map and everything."

"Perhaps she just gave up and left her pack where she dropped it," the first mage shrugged. "Better take it and leave it with Master Callum. He'll know what to do."

His companion nodded. "Good thinking. We can't just leave it here in the hallway for people to fall over in the middle of the night."

"Indeed not brother," the first mage agreed as they started to head off. "Can't have people falling over and breaking their necks in the middle of the night can we. I tell you what though, I don't envy Master Callum the difficult decisions he's going to have to make. Just think what the council will say after today's events…"

As the two mages moved away Phae took a massive gasp of air. She had come within a hair's breadth of being detected and worse luck had lost her pack in the process.

She looked once more at her bed chamber door and considered turning back. As the pain in her head faded she clenched her teeth. No, she wouldn't turn back this time. It really was now or never.

Half an hour later, with two small packages of food clutched tightly in her invisible hands, Phae hurried through the lower hallways of the Citadel. Though for now at least she remained concealed under a veil of magic, she stuck to the shadows as best she could. She could sense already it was only a few hours until dawn, and if she wasn't quick, she might miss her chance to escape through the portal.

She arrived at the council chamber and looked down the stone staircase revealed at its centre. Discovered by her parents long before she was born, the stairway led into a secret sanctum that had once been used by the 'Isle's previous rulers, a corrupt group of mages known as the Inner Circle. Though they had for the most part now been defeated, and their few surviving members scattered across the land, their sanctum still remained, and in it, her planned means of escape.

When they had first opened up the hidden sanctum, her parents had discovered, among other curiosities, an ancient portal to the mainland that the sanctum's inhabitants had used to conceal their movements from the mages in the chamber above. Since her father had ordered the sanctum emptied of its contents for study, he had set up a small research team especially tasked with trying to decipher the portal's ancient runes and trying to find a way – somehow – to alter its destination. At present, according to Lena, the portal came out a few miles south of Pegwell. It certainly beat getting a boat to the mainland that was for sure.

Cautiously, Phae descended the cold stone steps. Thankfully someone had installed a set of magical lanterns to light the way. As the sanctum was now supposedly open to anyone, the heavy-set doors were wide open. Phae paused, and held her breath. If anyone was still awake at this ungodly hour they almost *deserved* to spot her, but then, she was still invisible...

Silently, she crept past the steel doors into an expansive hallway lined with statues on either side. Her target was on the far end of the winding corridor, in what most explorers might think was a storeroom. Of course, she knew better. She arrived at her destination to find the portal-room wide open and a group of mages slumped over in their chairs, snoring peacefully amidst piles of parchments, books and experimental apparatus. It had clearly been another long night of labour.

Breathing slowly, Phae crept into the room, doing her best to avoid the bowls of half-eaten dinner and stacks of books that blocked her path. She had taken no more than two steps when all of a sudden, the pain returned. She let out a small yelp, then grimaced as she tried desperately to avoid emitting any more sound. As she did so, the female mage closest to her started to stir. Phae winced as pain wracked through her skull. Something was changing inside her, she could feel it, but right now she didn't know what. Given the events of the past few days, she expected the worst.

Then it happened.

With a flash, the portal room was suddenly bathed in light. Phae looked down at her hands and saw not only that she was no longer invisible, but the light was coming from within her!

In a matter of moments all three mages were wide awake and on their feet.

"What's going on here?"

"Who are you?"

"What time is it?"

Phae screamed. With the thoughts of one condemned to certain capture, she made one final burst for freedom. Shoving the nearest woman down into her chair, Phae burst past the three sets of outreaching arms and made a dive towards the portal.

It was only a few steps away.

Three… two… one…

All of a sudden, the sanctum disappeared and nausea swept over her. It felt as if the world itself had been turned on its head. A few seconds of discomfort and she suddenly found herself standing atop a small rise overlooking a vast expanse of farmland. All around her the countryside of the north-west coast was illuminated by her incandescence.

Phae began to panic. It would only be a matter of moments before someone decided to come through the portal after her, and here she was, a shining beacon in the midst of the darkness.

In a fit of panic, Phae started to run.

3

The night was still dark and the city streets still thick with fog by the time Callum descended from his tower to hurry to the far side of the city, right by the city wall, to the small place his two dear friends called home.

In any other city in the whole Kingdom, to walk the streets alone at this hour would be asking for trouble, but here in Asturia, things weren't quite the same as they were on the mainland. People came to the Magical Isle voluntarily – of their own free will – and in so doing, agreed to abide by the charter that had been set in place in order to keep the city streets safe. Of course, after all that had happened with the treachery of the Inner Circle, Callum had had to have the charter amended somewhat from its old, authoritarian style, but the principle was still the same; Asturia would be a safe-haven for all who wanted to keep it that way, and if you didn't like it, you were asked to leave.

Naturally, there were still patrols that watched the streets and patrolled the coast beyond the city walls, but other than the odd incident every few years, Asturia was perhaps the safest place Callum could imagine for anyone to live.

This in mind, he nodded his greeting as he was saluted by a small group of watch-men and women patrolling the city centre. Though he could appreciate their surprise at seeing him rushing through the streets, he didn't stop to say hello or see how they fared. Instead he continued on at pace through the open square of the market district on into the narrower streets where many of the 'Isle's more "long term" residents lived.

Knowing the route like the back of his hand, it didn't take him long to navigate his way through the warren of side-streets and alleyways to the large brown door that marked the entrance to his friends' home. Above the door was marked the inscription "wisdom exalteth her children and layeth hold of them that seek her". Very Lena, he thought to himself fondly. She always had been the clever one.

Taking a tentative step forward, he rapped on the door.

No one answered.

He knocked again, this time louder.

Still no response.

Just as he considered calling out and knocking for a third time, he heard the sound of movement and someone stumbling their way to the door. A loud bang followed by a curse and a grumble told him Aaron was clumsily making his way to the door. His magical sight was so powerful these days Callum sometimes forgot that his best friend was effectively blind to the "real" world.

Another grumble and the figure behind the door started rattling with a number of bolts and chains. Though the Magical Isle was without doubt one of the safest places to live in the whole Kingdom, Lena always did like to be careful.

Eventually, after what seemed like an awful lot of rattling and grumbling, the door was opened a crack and a familiar face peered out.

"Who is it? This better be important – do you know what time it is?!"

Callum stepped forward. "Open the door Aaron, it's me."

"Callum? I should have known it would be *you* disturbing me. Never could let me get a good night's sleep could you!"

Callum couldn't help but smile as Aaron opened the door wider and beckoned him in. He always did like to grumble. "This better be worth it." Callum stepped inside. "Tea?"

Callum nodded and followed obediently as Aaron led him through the house, past a small study, and on through into the kitchen. As was always the way, Aaron kept a good supply of biscuits. He reached for the tin. "Want one?" he asked. Callum just shook his head. Aaron shrugged and took one for himself before lighting the stove and preparing the tea. Callum helped himself to a seat.

"What's so important that it couldn't wait until the morning eh? If I had known it was you I probably wouldn't have been so quick in rushing to the door!" Though he joked, Callum could detect a subtle undertone of concern in his friend's voice. Typical Aaron.

"Well I've been thinking–"

"Oh no, here we go…"

"About Phae."

"Oh."

"I take it you heard about what happened yesterday?"

"Kind of hard *not* to hear about it if I'm honest with you. It is true about Kulgrim?"

"Afraid so," Callum sighed. He accepted the cup of tea his friend offered him gratefully. He took a sip. "You know I was worried something like this would happen. Worried someone would get hurt – I mean *really* hurt."

Aaron remained silent as Callum put his tea down on the table and rested his head in his hands. He began to massage his temples with his fingers. "I just don't know what to do Aaron. She's only a girl."

"A girl with very unique parentage," Aaron added.

"A girl with very unique parentage," Callum agreed. "Who through no real fault of her own just burnt down the Halls of Meditation and killed a man in the process. They were Halls of *Meditation* Aaron – she wasn't even supposed to be practising magic!" He sighed. "She's getting out of control. I just don't know what to do…"

Aaron laid a hand on his friend's shoulder as he took a sip of tea. Just then a bleary-eyed figure came to stand at the doorway. She wore a dressing gown wrapped tightly around her. She came in and sat down beside them. "Oh, it's you Callum. Can't sleep either eh?" she said, taking the cup of tea Aaron offered her with a polite nod of thanks. "I'd only just got off to sleep myself."

"You heard then?"

"About Phae? Yes, I had heard some rumours. That wasn't why I couldn't sleep though. I've been having these really strange dreams recently. Really not nice."

Callum let out another sigh. "Tell me about it," he said. "For over a week now I've barely had a wink of sleep. There's something not quite right in the realm, though for the life of me yet I can't figure out what."

"Have you been to the Seer about it?"

"Not yet." Callum shook his head. "I've been kind of preoccupied with other matters…"

"Poor girl," Lena sighed. "And it doesn't help her mother isn't around much to help. Have you heard from Kiera at all?"

"She sent a message a week or so ago now saying she might be making progress tracking down the last members of the Inner Circle. She thinks she's getting somewhere but I'm not so sure."

"Do you think the Lintari will ever find them?" Aaron asked.

Callum shrugged. "I don't honestly know," he replied. "If there's one thing I will say about this island's former masters, it's that they really know how to stay out of sight."

"Well they've had centuries of experience at it I guess," Aaron said wearily, "crafty buggers."

"I'm afraid you're right there my friend," Callum nodded, taking another sip of tea. He shook his head as Aaron again offered him a biscuit. "I'm afraid the longer this hunt goes on the more likely it is we'll never find them. It's been over twenty years now…"

Aaron tutted. "Twenty years," he said slowly, looking towards Lena, "can you really believe it's been twenty years already?"

Lena raised an eyebrow but remained silent. Somewhere below the surface Callum was sure he could sense some tension. He had known for some time now Lena wanted to get married but Aaron still hadn't summoned the courage to propose. He made a mental note to speak to him about it later.

After a long moment's pause, Lena finally spoke. "So anyway," she said, "this still doesn't solve the problem we have with Phae. Nor indeed does it answer our questions about the strange dreams we've been having. It seems there's only really one solution at this moment in time to me…"

Aaron knew what was coming. His expression was pained. "Oh, do we have to?"

Lena nodded firmly. "Yes we do have to Aaron. It will do you good to speak to the Seer again after your last little falling out."

Callum shot her a questioning look. "He's been arguing with Elidor again has he?"

"You could say that yes, though arguing is perhaps not the right word."

"Aaron?"

"What?!" Aaron looked indignant. "I only made a comment about his weather forecasts – which I note Lena, he got wrong *yet again*. He's really not as good as he used to be you know."

"Well you could have been a bit more tactful about it, couldn't you?"

"Aaron? Tactful?" Callum snorted.

"That's enough from you Mister Mage," Aaron wagged his finger in Callum's general direction. "It's not easy being nice to the Seer when he's so grumpy all the time."

"So, you've noticed it as well have you?" Callum asked.

"Who hasn't? He's just so morbid these days. Every time I see him he seems to be in a worse mood than before. It's almost like he's got a death-wish or something."

With these words the conversation drew to a close. Death-wish or not, when the sun rose, they would all have to go and visit the Seer.

* * *

With the coming of dawn, the fog that enveloped the city finally began to fade, and the streets gradually warm to the light of the new day. As the hour approached something like respectable, Callum and his two friends ate a quick breakfast and headed out to the Citadel where they knew the Seer would already be hard at work. Crossing the wide stone bridge that led up to the Citadel's entrance they hurried on through reception to the spacious chamber that the Seer had turned into his personal office. As they arrived they found their old friend standing outside waiting patiently for them.

"Ah there you are, I've been waiting long enough for the three of you. Good morning Callum, Lena... Aaron."

The three companions greeted the Seer warmly, though Aaron slightly less so as he watched for sign of reproach from the Seer for their previous falling out. Even after the many years they had known Elidor, none of them could quite get used to his unnatural ability to know when they wanted to see him. "I take it you were looking for me?"

Though a formality given he knew they were coming, the question did much to put them at their ease. They followed him into the chamber in which he was working. He picked up a half-finished cup of herbal tea from the side of his desk and drained it in a single gulp. "I would offer you some, but I know none of you want any," he said. "Please do take a seat."

Callum shifted a pile of papers from a chair in the far corner of the room and dragged it over to the Seer's desk. Ever since he had returned from his exile in the mountains and Callum had offered him the job of Island Administrator, the Seer had progressively taken on more and more tasks until now they could all see he was stretched too far. As the companions took their seats Elidor remained standing and paced the room anxiously in a manner most out of character. Callum frowned.

"Are you alright Elidor?"

The Seer stopped in his tracks and snapped round. "Alright? Yes, why – do you think something is wrong?"

"Well that's why we came to see you," Callum replied. "The dreams..."

"Ah yes the dreams," Elidor nodded. As he spoke, he started to pace again. Aaron was just about to say something but Lena grabbed his arm just in time. In his current state of mind, it didn't bode well to rile the Seer any further. "So, you've all been having them too I take it?"

"Well Callum and I have," Lena replied.

The Seer turned to Aaron. "And you?"

"I haven't had any just yet," Aaron replied, "I'm just here to keep the other two company."

"Quite."

Lena interceded quickly. "So, what do you know about the dreams Elidor? What have you seen?"

Elidor stopped his pacing and gazed out his office window. He mulled Lena's words over in his head. "What have I seen? I regret to say I have seen a great deal my friends." He sighed. "Unfortunately, most of my visions of late have been blurred – distorted even. Never in all my long years have I experienced anything like it. Either my powers have become corrupted in some way, or they are fading completely. My sight is becoming less predictable the day and I am at a loss as to the reason why."

"No change there then," Aaron muttered to himself.

"Aaron!" Lena hit him on the arm.

"I'm afraid that while he might not mean it as an insult, our friend Aaron is right to feel aggrieved. As I have told the three of you in the past, my sight often works in mysterious ways. I see glimpses of the future – or possible futures – that gain in frequency and accuracy as the vision nears its resolution. My concern is that of late my visions have been blurred or distorted – in some things they have dried up completely. All I see beyond the month now is darkness. It concerns me…"

"So, you have no idea what these dreams we've been having could mean?" Callum asked.

The Seer shook his head solemnly. Callum took a deep breath. A Seer without foresight was like a mage without magic. He could see the lines of concern etched in Elidor's face. "I haven't a clue," he said softly. "All I can offer the three of you is this: be concerned, be very concerned. I have not known this type of uncertainty since the time I first encountered the three of you and your friend Kiera. Not since Varrus–" The Seer's voice grew choked. Lena stood up and put her arm around him. With his visions fading the Seer was as a lame man having his crutches taken away. The Seer's life had been a constant struggle with the curse of his "gift", and yet now without it he was both scared and very, very alone. Lena did her best to reassure him.

"There, there Elidor don't worry. The four of us will be sure to be on our guard for whatever's created this disturbance in the world of magic. The four of us..."

"*Four*?" Aaron looked up.

"Sorry, I forget myself," Lena sighed. Like Callum and Aaron, she hadn't seen Kiera in months. "The *three* of us..."

Just then the Seer's eyes snapped wide open. He looked towards Callum. Only one word passed his lips: "Five."

"Five?"

Elidor shook his head as if to try and clear it of confusion. "I think Callum, it's time you went to check on your daughter."

Callum shot the Seer a look of concern. "Phae? What about her?"

"I can't tell you why my friend, but something tells me you need to go see her right this very moment."

The three friends didn't need telling twice. In a matter of heartbeats Callum, Aaron and Lena were all running for the door...

* * *

It took them only a few minutes to reach Phae's bed chamber, and before they had even reached her door Callum knew what they would find – or more precisely, what they wouldn't. He stared wide-eyed and open-mouthed at the empty room, the contents of Phae's desk and cupboards scattered across the floor. Near her bed he saw the shattered remains of the photo frame he had bought her for her birthday. The family portrait was missing.

"Lena, are any ships due to sail this morning?"

"None that I know of, why?"

"You don't think she's taken a ship, do you?" Aaron asked.

"Well not if there aren't any ships due to sail," Callum said as he searched desperately among the discarded items on the floor for some form of clue. "There's only one place she could have gone."

"You don't think she'd really go through with it, do you? I mean she's tried and failed before."

"Look at it!" Callum raised his voice and swept his arm to encompass the whole bed chamber. His voice was choked. Tears were already forming in the corners of his eyes. "Someone has *died* Aaron. I should have been there for her. I should have…"

He turned to look for his friend but found Aaron had already made for the door. Lena grabbed his arm and pulled him along after them. "Come on Callum. If we're quick we might yet catch her."

4

Phae ran for her life.

She didn't even know if any mages had followed her through the portal, but a deep, primal force told her to keep on running.

She followed a path heading roughly eastwards before it came to an end and she continued her journey cross-country. Every so often a sharp pain would take her by surprise and she would find herself disappearing, or perhaps running twice as fast, or even at times not even running at all but floating in the direction she wished to head. Her magics were out of control and there was no knowing when they might change again and increase the chances of her capture. At least she wasn't a shining beacon of light anymore.

Reaching a small copse of trees, Phae stopped at the first tree she reach and leaned against it, panting hard. Far in the distance to the east she could just make out the first rays of dawn breaking on the horizon which meant it wouldn't be long before her father learnt of her disappearance and started on her trail. She looked down into her hands to see what meagre packages of food she had managed to keep hold of as she ran. She must have dropped at least half her supplies on the way, which didn't bode well for her when all the wizards in the realm might be on her trail, but she would just have to make do.

As her breathing slowed and her heart stopped beating so loudly she greedily set to work devouring the first of her food parcels. Only one packet. If she was really careful, she might just make it to the Lake in that time.

She turned now towards the west in search of any sign of pursuit. Though she couldn't see anyone on her trail just yet, she didn't want to take any risks. She turned to face the north-east – a direction she knew from memory would lead her towards the Lake. Without a second thought, she continued on her way.

* * *

Hours passed, and as they did so the last of Phae's energy reserves were gradually depleted. The sun was nearing its midday peak and before she knew what had come over her, she ravenously finished off the last of her rations. She dearly would have loved a sip of water, but she had lost her water-skin when she had lost her pack, and she was a long way from anywhere she could get another. Only the distant possibility of the enchanted Lake offered any hope of quenching her thirst, and that was still another day's travel away.

A wave of tiredness swept over her. Though she knew she had a long way to go, she couldn't help but find herself drifting slowly, inexorably, into a deep, deep sleep…

* * *

In a flash of brilliant golden light Varrus, dark emissary of the destroyer-of-worlds returned from death to walk once more in the realm of those who drew breath. Lightning crackled and sparks of magical energy cascaded from the heavens to bring him back from his hidden purgatory at the behest of the evil star-god.

In a heartbeat the lightning stopped and the shower of sparks ceased. His body aching and weak, Varrus took a tentative step forward and surveyed the land before him. He was in the realm of men once more. In the distance he could make out the neat rectangular outlines of human farms with outbuildings scattered between them. If he strained his sight hard enough he could just make out the shapes of men and women working the fields.

He took a deep breath of the warm summer air. There had been a fog recently – and probably a storm too – for the air was still damp from the mist. Goodness it felt good to be alive again – to be able to breathe, to smell.

Varrus' hand instinctively reached for his belt. He was grateful to find the magical sword Nu'ra still at his side. It had cost him a great deal to obtain the fabled sword, and though the Lintari now had its twin, it remained one of the most potent weapons in the realm. He caressed its hilt as he began to search for an unwitting victim.

Though outwardly at least he appeared the same as he did in his former life, he could sense he wasn't quite the same as he once was. His reserves of magic were vastly depleted and he knew he would have to obtain more if he was to return to his former strength. Not that he had *ever* been beyond murder to take the power he needed...

Just then a scent reached him that was at once familiar to him, yet at the same time slightly different. It pulled him in the direction of a small outcrop of trees less than a mile off. Something told him what he'd find when he got there would make his journey more than worthwhile.

Slowly, carefully, he took another step forward. As he did so he felt his whole body creak under the effort of movement. It had been far too long since he had last walked in the land of mortals, yet with each step he felt the life of old returning to his ancient limbs, filling him with a vigour he had not felt for centuries. Not since he first took the robes of the mage under the tutelage of the corrupt wizards of Asturia had he felt so much energy – so much *love* – for life.

So, this is what it feels to be alive!

He gasped as he spotted the curled-up form of a young girl sleeping deeply in a small alcove beside a tree. Her thin, fragile frame made her look perhaps anything up to five years younger than she really was, but even without the majority of his former powers, Varrus could sense he was confronted by a creature of supreme power.

He stared thoughtfully at the girl; watched intently the slow rhythmic movements of her chest as she breathed. He took a step closer to her. She didn't stir. He took another step, and then another. He leaned over her until he was so close he could feel her breath on his cheek. So close now he could see just how small and fragile she really was – a being of awesome power trapped in the body of a young girl.

Scared. She was scared alright – he could smell it. The smell of fear hung like a musk on her body that pleased him and told him how best he could exploit her.

I wonder what she's doing here…

Varrus considered the young girl more closely now. He drew in a deep lungful of her own expended air and tasted it on the tip of his tongue. There was something familiar in her scent – that much was clear – but there was something else too, something in the way she looked.

The girl slept so deeply Varrus didn't give second thought to turning her head gently in his hand so she faced him fully and he could stare intently at her slumbering features. He gasped as a hint of recognition dawned on him.

"It can't be," he muttered to himself. "Surely not…"

He examined the girl once more. The scent certainly matched, and the power did too now he thought about it.

A cruel smile formed on his thin lips as he realised the true value of his prize. Skargyr had been most generous in his gift, and most meticulous in his plan. Varrus would not let such a precious gift go to waste.

Slowly, carefully, he reached towards the slumbering form…

* * *

In the land of her dreams, Phae screamed.

Every way she turned fire blazed around her, encircling her and keeping her pinned to the spot. In the distance she could hear a faint voice crying from somewhere amidst the flame. She wanted to help but she couldn't. The fire just wouldn't let her.

Voices swirled around her, faces forming in the thick smoke that billowed from the flames and tried to choke her.

"It's all your fault!" Master Kulgrim spat at her. "I am dead because of you!"

"It's all your fault Phae." The face of her mother took form now, circling her alongside Kulgrim – taunting her, urging her to throw herself upon the flames.

"I didn't mean to hurt anyone!" she cried.

"You never do though do you." The face of her father now materialised in the smoke. The heat of the flames was getting intense now. She could barely muster the strength to stand. "Admit it child: you're a *failure*!"

"Yes child – a failure!" her mother agreed. "All you do is bring pain and suffering wherever you go."

"Failure!" Kulgrim echoed. "Weak! And after all the things your parents have done for you."

"You don't deserve to live Phae," her father said. "We should never have brought you into the world."

"Never," her mother agreed. "Come now Phae, be a good girl and jump in the fire. You'd be doing us all a favour."

"Go on Phae: do it!" Kulgrim cackled.

"Yes Phae, do it." The distant voices of her friends and fellow students joined the chorus, urging her to jump in the fire and die. Phae's eyes were wide and glazed over in fear. She searched desperately for a friendly face; someone – anyone – who she might cling to for support.

Tears flooded from her eyes as somewhere out of the smoke a single dark, malignant voice called out to her and beckoned her forward. At the voice's command the flames abruptly ceased to burn and the smoke faded. Though the voice made her feel instinctively uneasy, there was something deeply comforting about its presence.

A dark robed figure strode out of the mist and held out his hand to her.

"Take my hand child and follow me. I'll help you keep these nasty dreams at bay…"

5

It had been a long time since he had last used the portal to the mainland. He had almost forgotten just how strange it could feel stepping from one world into another. Indeed, the sudden shock of the transition caused Callum to take a step backwards as he appeared on the rise overlooking the farmland of the coast. As he did so he was nearly knocked over by Aaron who followed close behind.

"Oi, watch it would you!"

Callum turned to apologise and then quickly pulled his friend aside as Lena followed them through last of all. Unlike the two men, she emerged from the portal completely unflustered. She took a look around her.

"Well I must say it's been a long time since I've been here," she said. "I must have used the portal only a handful of times since we discovered it."

Callum nodded. He knew all too well how Lena preferred to travel by sea. He couldn't see it himself – he never did get on with boats.

He clapped his hand on Aaron's shoulder as his friend narrowed his eyes and scanned the countryside for any sign of a clue.

"What do you see?"

Aaron frowned. "Not much I'm afraid. Her magical residue is faint, which would suggest we're already at least five or six hours behind her. It's hard to follow but at best guess I'd say she's heading east."

"She is," Lena nodded, pointing to a section of flattened grass leading off down the rise. "There's a trail look."

Callum went over to investigate. He crouched down and examined the path Lena pointed to. Amidst the flattened grasses a set of footprints led the way east. Judging by the distance between each footprint, she had been travelling at quite some pace. Callum suggested this to his friends and they both agreed.

"Makes sense," Lena said, "she's running scared."

Callum took a deep breath and rose to his feet. "Right, we better get moving – and fast. If we hurry we might just catch her before the day is out."

With that they set off at a canter, Aaron leading them down the crest heading east through pastures and fields as the sun slowly rose to its midday peak. For much of the way the trail was fairly simple to follow – Phae had cared little for masking sign of her path – but whenever they came upon a point where the trail seemed to fade and they veered off course, Aaron's powers were strong enough that they never left the trail for long and always quickly re-joined the path.

As the sun reached its zenith, they finally drew to a stop to take their bearings. They were all breathing hard. Beads of sweat ran down Callum's face.

"I can't believe she's gone so far," he panted, "I guess she really meant it this time."

Lena frowned as she scanned the landscape ahead of them. Thus far they had encountered only a handful of people on their journey, and none had caught sight of Phae. Still, the path was clear enough. "She's got to have stopped to rest at some point," Lena said finally. Like her companions she too was quite out of breath from their morning exertions and was pleased for the brief respite. "We must be catching her by now surely," she said. "Aaron?"

Aaron looked up from where he stood with his hands braced against his knees, sucking in deep gasps of air. Of the three companions he seemed – surprisingly – the most out of shape. He examined the trail again with his magical vision. "We're still at least five hours behind her," he said with a shake of his head. "Probably more even. Her signature is still there, but it's really faded." He drew a deep breath and glanced over to where Callum stood staring worriedly into the distance. "I don't suppose you brought any provisions with you did you Callum?"

Callum turned and shook his head. "Sorry, I didn't think to. I honestly didn't expect us to be gone this long."

"No chance of us stopping off to get a quick bite to eat then?"

Again, Callum shook his head. "If there's any chance at all of our catching her before evening we need to keep pressing on. She's got to have stopped at some point…"

Aaron was about to make some grumbling comment about his stomach and not having agreed to traipse halfway across the west coast, but his conscience held his tongue. Though his friend tried to put on a brave face, he could sense the turmoil and despair weighing heavy on Callum's heart. In all the time he'd known him, he'd never known his friend brought so low. Lena squeezed his arm reassuringly as the companions made ready to continue on the trail. She too could see Callum stood at the precipice of a very deep and dark abyss.

They travelled hard for the rest of the day, pushing on well into the first hours of twilight until Callum was forced to concede that they had gone as far as they could and needed to find somewhere to rest. At one point it had seemed they might have been closing in on Phae's trail, but now the light faded, there seemed no chance at all of them catching her with the remaining light of day.

It was with some reluctance then that Callum led his friends towards a small hamlet, the lights from which they could just make out in the far distance. As they drew closer he was shocked to find they had somehow, miraculously stumbled upon a place familiar to him, a place he and Lena had been once before. Though the location held only the very darkest memories for the two mages, the sight of the warm lights of the newly rebuilt hamlet of Keln was a welcome one.

As they drew closer and Lena recognised where it was Callum was leading them, she shot him a surprised look, but he just shrugged and continued to lead them in. When she told Aaron where it was they were headed he couldn't help but let out a yelp of surprise.

"Keln?!"

Lena nodded.

"But I thought the place was burned down, you know, after you and Callum…"

Lena grabbed his arm. "Shush… Callum will hear you! We don't need you reminding him what happened here." She lowered her voice, "Especially not now."

"But I thought it didn't exist anymore. Callum burnt it down didn't he?"

Callum, who had caught the drift of his friends' conversation, turned to look at them. "I did," he said simply. "Some of the local traders were keen to rebuild it; I thought I'd lend a hand."

"So, you knew about this?"

Callum nodded as they drew upon the outer perimeter of the hamlet. Already they could hear the sound of music and much singing emerging from the local tavern. Callum led them to the door. "I knew it was being rebuilt, but I didn't know they had worked so fast. In all honesty I didn't realise we were so close to this place – it didn't occur to me we had come so far. Strange how things work out really."

"Coincidence, or fate?" Aaron said provocatively. "I wonder what the Seer would say."

"Oh, don't you start on the Seer again!" Lena scolded. "Come on Callum," she said as she pushed the tavern door open, "I think it's about time we ordered some food."

They entered the tavern to find it almost exactly the same as the original, complete with raging fire and low ceiling. Aaron banged his head on a low beam as they entered. He swore vigorously.

"You'd think they'd have sorted that out when they rebuilt the place," he said dryly. "What a stupid place to put a roof support."

"I think it's part of the 'aesthetic'," Callum said absently. "Come on, let's find a table."

The three companions worked their way across the busy tavern to a small table in the corner. As the barmaid came over to take their order a glint of recognition shone in her eyes.

"Excuse me sir, I hope you don't mind me asking, but do I recognise you from somewhere? Your face seems awful familiar to me but for the life of me I just can't place it."

Callum looked up from his menu and at once the barmaid said excitedly, "Ah it *is* you! You're the one who helped fund the rebuilding work now aren't you?"

Lena raised an eyebrow and looked at Callum. "'Fund'?"

Aaron also shot him a quizzical look. "'Sir'?!"

"It's a long story, I'll explain later."

"You never said you *funded* the place Callum."

"Well maybe I did a little. It seemed only right after–"

The barmaid cut him off. "So, it *is* you! Well my-oh-my, wait till Mary hears about this!" Callum made to hand the barmaid a few coins from his pocket. "Oh, don't you worry about that sir. Can't have the saviour of Keln paying for food and board here!" She hurried off to see to their order.

It was now Aaron's turn to raise an eyebrow. "'Saviour of Keln'? I know you like fame Callum but *really*?" He chuckled to himself. "You really are a local hero aren't you."

"I was only trying to help!" Callum pleaded. "And besides, you'd have done the same thing given the chance."

"Don't worry Callum, I think it's a really nice thing you've done for the people here," Lena said reassuringly. Callum shot her an appreciative look.

Aaron continued to chuckle. "My-oh-my, 'saviour of Keln'. Whatever next eh?!"

Though they had never intended to rely upon the hospitality of the good people of Keln, Callum, Aaron and Lena had a most refreshing evening after their long day on the road. Aaron especially was delighted when the barmaid offered up desert as well "on the house", though Callum remained reserved and solemn throughout. While he and his two friends ate heartily and rested in the best rooms the tavern had to offer, his thoughts were constantly drawn back to Phae and the misery she was likely suffering in some field or wood somewhere, cold and alone.

While Aaron and Lena retired for the night, Callum lay for hours on his bed, staring up at the ceiling, mulling over all that had happened and the path that now lay before him. Was Elidor right – was there really a major shift in the world of magic? If there was, it certainly explained a lot of things, but where did this leave *him*? And what of Phae? It couldn't be coincidence surely, that she had run away at such a crucial moment as this?

Callum squeezed his eyes tight shut and tried to block out his wild thoughts for a few brief moments. Nothing he did seemed to work. It was going to be a very long night.

What was it old Kulgrim had always said? *Magic works in strange ways...*

* * *

The three companions emerged from their rooms at the crack of dawn, Aaron rubbing his bleary eyes and complaining bitterly to Lena for having woken him so early. Callum smiled as he appreciated his friend's efforts to distract him from his worries, though truth be told even just an hour's sleep would have been a blessing.

Lena studied him as they made their way downstairs for breakfast. Already Aaron was ahead of them taking the stairs two at a time.

"No sleep eh?"

Callum shook his head.

Lena put her arm around him. "It'll be alright you know. We'll find her Callum don't you worry. She's scared that's all – and who wouldn't be with all that's happened of late."

Callum turned to her, trying his very best to find some comfort in her words. Yet however much he tried he just couldn't summon the courage to believe her. He lowered his voice: "What am I going to do Lena? What will Kiera say? I've been an awful parent I know – Phae deserves better than this – but I've tried my best I really have. I've lost my daughter, and soon I'll lose my wife as well when she finds out what's happened. I've failed Lena, I–"

From the bottom of the stairs a familiar voice called up to them. "Are you two coming or what? Some of us are hungry you know."

Despite himself, Callum could help but let out a small laugh. Lena sighed. "Some things really do never change," she said. "Come on Callum, we'll never hear the end of it if we're late for breakfast. We've got a long day ahead of us, and if yesterday was anything to go by, we'll need all the energy we can get…"

They breakfasted quickly, before arranging with the landlady some provisions for the coming day. Sensibly, Lena took Aaron to the local shops and with what little coin she had, acquired them some packs, a couple of water-skins, and a few other camping essentials. Though she dearly hoped they'd find Phae within the day, it wouldn't do for them not to be prepared for the worst.

They met Callum back outside the tavern only a short while later. While they did their best to cheer him up, the sight of the packs and extra provisions Lena had purchased did little to ease his mood.

They left Keln in strained silence, picking up the trail where it left off, following it as it turned suddenly towards the north. As soon as it did, they all knew precisely where Phae was headed.

Callum's voice was barely a whisper, "The Lake."

6

Phae opened her eyes and found that she floated in a world of grey. The mysterious robed figure who had saved her from the awful nightmare still held her by the hand, and led her firmly on towards the sanctuary of Lake Forever.

He had promised a great many things when he had first taken her by the hand, and foremost amongst his promises was to take her to the Lake. He said he knew a way to make the pain go away completely. If there was even the slightest truth in what the strange man said, he was worth following, Phae thought to herself, realising as she did that even if she did want to leave him, he wouldn't be letting go of her any time soon. His voice was just so alluring, so captivating, and if his promises weren't enough, the vice-like grip he exerted upon her small hand was far, far stronger than she had strength to escape from. She was, for the time being at least, trapped in his control.

He turned and scowled at her as she threatened to lag behind.

"Come on girl there's not much further to go now – we're almost at the forest's edge."

Phae continued to follow on behind him in silence. He tugged harder at her arm. "Come on, don't slow down now, we're almost there."

Phae sighed and allowed the strange man to continue to pull her along. As promised, they soon neared the edge of the forest that marked the Lake's surrounds. Tall trees, drawn in this bleary landscape in hues of black and grey stood sentinel over the forest's entrance. Though the world she inhabited felt more like a dream than anything else, a small voice at the back of her head wondered if this really was the case. She watched intently as her robed companion reached out to touch one of the strange trees. He shivered in delight as life-energy coursed into his body.

"The Lake's guardians have lost none of their energy I see," he muttered. Phae gasped as the tree slowly started to wither before her eyes.

They took another few steps into the forest and the process was repeated. Another tree died. Phae struggled to free herself from the robed figure's grip.

"Oh, do behave girl. Only a few more of these and I shall have the power to guide you in your task. You do want the pain to go away don't you?" With these words, a sharp spike of pain stabbed her in the temple. She clutched at her head with her free hand and cried out.

"Yes, yes, make it stop!"

"Good." The robed figure shot her a sinister smile. The agony in her head suddenly stopped. "I knew you'd soon learn to cooperate."

Phae was just about to cry out again when a small needle of discomfort warned her off. "I wouldn't do that if I were you. Come now girl, this won't take long…"

It did take long. It took hours upon hours. The distance between the forest's edge and the Lake itself seemed far greater than young Phae might have imagined, and though she was sure her captor had had his fill of life-energy from the trees, each new species or particularly large specimen they encountered drew them towards it and she was forced to watch helplessly as it slowly died to his withering touch. Through her contact with him, Phae could sense he was a mage – and a powerful one at that.

Again, she struggled to free herself of his grip. "Leave the trees alone!" she cried, "Can't you see they've had enough!"

Her dark-robed captor cursed and shot her an evil look. "Oh, do be quiet girl. You really are your father's daughter aren't you; he never did know when to give up."

Phae gasped. "My… my father? You know my father?" Her abductor remained silent. She kicked him in the shin. "Tell me!"

The dark mage yelped in pain. "How did you– Oh wait never mind. I see you're going to prove a nuisance aren't you. Time for a rest I think…"

In the blink of an eye, Phae's world went blank.

She awoke to find herself suspended above the centre of the Lake, hovering precariously above the cold and murky waters. In the distance her captor, the yet unnamed mage, watched her closely from the bank. He grinned wickedly as he saw she had come to her senses.

His voice thundered within her head. *"Come now child, our first task is now at hand. Do this for me now and your troubles will soon be over."*

Phae started to tremble. She couldn't feel any of her limbs. "What have you done to me?! Why am I floating here? Put me back on the shore you evil–"

All of a sudden, she could feel the mage's presence inside her head.

Phae screamed.

"Hush, hush. That's no way to talk to your saviour and friend, now is it? I'm afraid I had to take control of your body briefly to bring you to your current position, as only you have the power necessary for what I need you to do. Be thankful that I could only use you for a few brief moments, otherwise I might have been tempted to control you completely. I have great experience in these matters you know." Flashes of the dark mage's memories flooded into Phae's head. Images from a time long before she was born filled her thoughts, and a great leader under the mage's control. The man had a name: Osmar.

"You are a wicked, wicked man!" Phae shrieked. She grew hysterical. "How could you do that to someone?!"

Phae felt a flood of warm emotion fill her body. *"Thank you for your kind words child – I do try my very best. But I fear we have talked long enough. Now to the task at hand…"*

Phae flinched. Her whole body went rigid. She could feel the sinister thoughts of the dark mage filling her mind.

She knew that from this moment on her actions were no longer her own.

"Try not to resist – it will only make the pain worse."

Phae whimpered softly as she felt the dark mage's thoughts will her arms to stretch out in front of her with her palms face down towards the depths of the Lake below. A well of energy started to build within her.

"Good… good. Keep it up girl."

Phae remained silent. She knew that to resist now would be to incur the mage's wrath. She knew too little of the powers within her to attempt to fight back. Deep in the recesses of her mind, she clung to the image of the family portrait that still resided in her pocket. Leaving home had been a very, very bad idea.

Her despairing thoughts sent a ripple through the magical plain.

"Mother! Father!"

A shock of pain from the mage quickly silenced her. She watched with mute horror as the material of the world itself seemed to bend and alter around her hands.

"Nearly there…"

The waters of the Lake started to stir. Some giant orb below her started to move in the water. Was it really rising to the surface?

Phae risked a glance down at her feet, and sure enough, amidst the grey of her perpetual half-sleep a giant sphere of dazzling colour slowly rose from beneath the Lake's surface. The sight sent shivers down her spine.

"See girl, that there is a source – one of the great funnels through which magic flows into the realm."

"What… what are you going to do to it?"

"You'll see."

The dark mage cackled as with a mighty splash of displaced water the source rose into the air before her. All at once, dozens of coloured ribbons of magic started to play between her fingers.

"Yes, yes that's it. Only a little bit longer now child – we're almost done."

Phae could feel her hands contorting into strange and complex shapes. She felt herself manipulating the magical bands and bending the fabric of the world around the orb. The power of the source washed over her: it warmed her; it caressed her. For the faintest of moments, she felt as if she just might have found the release she was looking for. For one brief moment, everything made sense.

And then it was gone.

In the blink of an eye the source waned and became as the trees: dead and lifeless. As the colour faded and the magic ceased to flow the source withered and shrank, until it was but the size of one of her clenched fists. The lifeless orb dropped into the Lake with a splash.

Strangely, she felt an awful lot better.

"That's it girl – our work here is done. Feels good, doesn't it? You'd better hurry back to the shore now. I'm not sure how much longer you will be able to support yourself there."

Phae looked towards the bank and saw the dark mage beckoning her towards him. Instinctively she allowed herself to be drawn towards his outstretched hand.

As his mind finally left her own his words had a strange effect upon her senses. "Hurry now girl. We can't tarry here too long. We have an awful long way to travel." He reached out to grab her and pull her onto the shore. As soon as he touched her, she knew once more that she was trapped. His iron grip dug into her frail arms.

"Where are we going? I've done all you've asked of me, haven't I? Can't I go now?"

The dark mage smiled wickedly. "Oh, I can't let you go just yet girl. You have far too much to offer. We still have two more sources to close and our next stop is far, far away in the south. You will cooperate with me, now won't you?"

Phae nodded nervously. To argue now would be to bring about more pain.

"Good, I'm glad you agree." The dark mage started leading her back towards the forest. "Come my girl, we have a lot to do and little time to do it in. My master can't be kept waiting any longer." He glanced at her with an assessing eye. "You seem tired. Perhaps it's time you had a little rest."

She was about to protest but she found that while she was in the mage's grasp, she was completely helpless. She was fully and completely in the dark mage's control.

In the blink of an eye, Phae's world went blank.

7

Callum's eyes snapped open. Something was wrong: very wrong.

He had been dozing fitfully by the embers of their small campfire. Just as he thought he might be getting off to sleep a strange feeling of emptiness roused him from his slumber.

Across the camp, Lena sat bolt upright. She glanced round the camp until her eyes finally settled on Callum.

"What on earth was that?"

"I don't know." Callum's face was etched with concern. "How do you feel?"

"Strange…" Lena replied, "It almost feels as if I'm floating outside of my body, but I'm not – I know I'm not. Does that seem strange to you?"

"It would if I didn't feel the same way myself," Callum said with a frown. "It's almost like a part of me is missing. I can think of no better way to explain it."

At the sound of his friends' voices, Aaron strode over from where he had been sitting on watch. "What's all this commotion then you two? What's up?"

"Well we're not sure," Lena said as he sat down next to her. She reached for his hand. "You didn't feel anything by any chance, did you?"

Aaron shook his head, "No, why?"

"Something's wrong and whatever it is it just sent a major shockwave through the magical plain."

"And yet it clearly wasn't strong enough for Aaron to be affected," Callum mused.

"Perhaps he just hasn't felt it yet?" Lena suggested. "Either way something *big* just happened. If even only a small portion of what the Seer said is true then this can only be the beginning."

Callum sighed and shook his head in disbelief. "First Phae and now this…" He shifted uncomfortably. "I don't know about the rest of you but I'm not sure I'm going to be able to get much more sleep tonight. You can get some rest if you want Aaron – I don't mind taking your watch."

Aaron nodded appreciatively and settled down close to the smouldering embers. Beside him, Lena hugged her knees tightly to her chest.

Whatever had just happened, Callum didn't think *any* magic user would be able to sleep now…

The remainder of the night passed slowly for Callum and Lena who both shared equally in the distinct feeling of loss that had settled upon them. As the first rays of dawn finally started to creep over the horizon, they were both relieved to make ready for another day of travel.

Aaron complained bitterly as Lena did her best to rouse him.

"Is it that time already?" he yawned, "Make yourself useful and start on breakfast would you Callum? I don't know about the rest of you but I–"

Suddenly he cut himself short. "What in the blazes?!"

Lena looked concerned. "What is it?"

"My sight: it's…"

"What?"

"Faded."

"Faded?" It was Callum's turn to look concerned. "What's wrong with it?"

Aaron sat up and rubbed his eyes. His expression changed for the worse. "I… don't know. The world looks different somehow – the colours are changed. It's hard to explain."

Callum looked to Lena. "Do you think this has anything to do with what happened last night?"

"It has to," she nodded and turned to face Aaron. "But the question is, why didn't you notice the change last night when we did?"

Aaron shrugged, "Well it's not always light in my world you know. The world changes at night just as it does for you. Perhaps," he said thoughtfully, "perhaps whatever it was that happened took a while to have an effect."

They paused as they each gathered their thoughts. Finally, Lena spoke. "Well whatever the cause of this change in magic we need to get to the bottom of it – and soon," she said. "As if there wasn't reason enough to find Phae this whole situation makes things twice as urgent. As soon as we've eaten, I think it's a good idea we set off straight away."

They all nodded their agreement.

It didn't take long for them to eat their makeshift breakfast. As soon as they'd gathered their few possessions they set off at pace on towards the Lake, pushing hard despite the protests of their aching legs. While Aaron's sight had been rather worryingly hampered by the recent turn of events, knowing where Phae was headed made things somewhat easier.

They continued on for much of the morning until their path brought them to the edge of the forest that marked the Lake's surrounds. As they drew nearer, they saw the first of the withered trees.

Lena gasped. "Oh my goodness!"

"What is it?" Aaron asked.

"That tree: it's… dead!"

"It's worse than dead," Callum added. "It's like it's had every last ounce of life sucked out of it."

"And there's another one behind it look," Lena pointed, "And another. It's a trail!" She gasped and turned to face Callum. "You don't think Phae's responsible for this do you?"

Callum struggled to keep a neutral expression. "I don't know," he said. The cold withered bark fell away at his touch. "Whoever or whatever it was that did this I fear we shall very soon find the answer." He strode decisively into the forest. "Come on," he said, "it's time we got to the bottom of all this."

They followed him closely as he led them along the trail of lifeless trees all the way to the Lake's edge. What they found when they got there was enough to make Callum fall to his knees. Even Aaron stopped and gasped in shock.

The Lake… was dead.

Gone was the magical aura that emanated from its heart. Gone too was the energy – the life – that filled the Lake's visitors with a sense of warmth and well-being. Instead the Lake had become nothing more than a vast lifeless pool.

Tears began to stream down Callum's face. "What has she done?!"

Neither Aaron nor Lena could find the words to comfort him. Even Aaron felt himself welling up.

"It's grey," he mumbled to himself, "so very, very grey." He paused. "It's like the magic of the Lake has been sucked out and left nothing but an empty shell.

"I think," Lena said finally, "we know what happened to your sight Aaron. I think we now know why Callum and I felt as if a part of our beings had been taken away from us."

Callum looked up and turned to face her. "The source."

Lena nodded solemnly. "Now I don't know what's happened to it or what made it the way it is, but either way this is *serious*. This must have been the change or the stirring Elidor hinted at."

"Perhaps," Aaron agreed, taking a step closer to her and putting his arms round her, "but what would make Phae do such a thing? She couldn't have done this on her own surely?"

Lena shook her head sadly. "I just don't know," she replied. "One thing is for sure though – we need to find her and we need to find her *now*. Whatever it is that's making her do this we need to stop her before she can do any more damage."

They turned back towards the forest. It was then that Lena spotted a second trail not too far from where they had come out. "Well at least we know the way she went," Lena said pointedly. "What can you make of the trail Aaron?"

"Not a great deal," he sighed. "If it was faint before it's even fainter now my sight has dimmed. Having said that…" He paused. "There definitely does seem to be something different about it. Either she has changed, or something about her has changed. It's either that or she is travelling with someone."

Callum's face was pained. "I don't know what's worse, the thought of someone forcing my daughter to do these awful things, or the thought she may be doing them of her own free will."

Lena took a step towards the forest. She called back to the others. "Come on you two. If we want to have any chance of catching her we can't be waiting around here feeling sorry for ourselves – we've got to get moving!"

Aaron tugged his friend by the arm. "She's right you know," he said. "We can't stand around here feeling sorry for ourselves. Your daughter needs us."

Callum gulped as the enormity of the situation started to sink in. The Seer had been right to be worried. They had to find Phae before it was too late.

8

In the long dark of her endless half-sleep, Phae drifted helplessly on her way.

The countryside rushed past beneath her feet. Up ahead the dark mage rode swiftly onwards, a long thick piece of rope trailing from his horse back to where she floated behind him, the rope tied with a thick knot round her waist. Wherever it was the dark mage planned to take her next, he sure was in a hurry.

"Don't look so miserable girl – you should count yourself lucky I'm not making you walk!"

Phae remained silent. She didn't know what to say. She never knew what to say anymore. She had already learnt that the mage knew her father. Of course, she knew the stories of how her parents had met and had defeated the evil schemes of the dark mage Varrus, but this couldn't be…

Her thoughts trailed off as up ahead the dark mage allowed his horse to slow and she found herself drifting closer towards him.

The dark mage drew to a halt. As he did so, Phae floated past him only to be jerked back by the strong rope. Varrus climbed down from his horse.

"Time for you to rest I think…"

With these words, once more, Phae's world went blank.

* * *

A fortnight passed – maybe even an entire month – she couldn't tell.

Each day was the same as the last. Every day she'd wake mid-morning to find she was still being dragged helplessly behind the dark mage's horse. After a few hours, they'd stop to rest and take on water before briskly continuing on their way. Hours and hours would then pass them by until finally the mage would draw to a halt, dismount, and send her back into the world of darkness.

Not that the world of grey is much better...

In a world stripped of colour the difference between night and day was meaningless. Just when she thought it might be day time, she'd spot things that would tell her otherwise: owls hunting in nearby woods; foxes out on patrol.

Was the mage really riding non-stop?

Certainly, the rate at which he got through horses suggested as much. She never quite got to see *how* he obtained them as she was always "asleep" when it happened. This was perhaps a small blessing given how he was likely to have taken them. She certainly didn't want any more deaths weighing on her mind.

She paused to consider the number of horses the dark mage had ridden to exhaustion and then abandoned, but when she got past a dozen, she started to lose count. However, one thing was for sure: she was now a very, *very* long way from home.

Just then, up ahead the dark mage started to slow. Phae braced herself for the impending jerking motion that would pull her to a stop as the rope reached its limit. It was never a pleasant experience.

The mage dismounted and walked over to her.

"Nearly there now girl. Nearly time for your second task."

With these words, once more Phae's world went blank.

* * *

Phae's eyes snapped open. As soon as they did she knew they had reached the end of their journey. Ten enormous monoliths rose up out of the darkness, surrounding them on all sides, hemming them in from the world beyond. Such was the size and majesty of the huge monolith structures she almost missed the small form of the dark mage a little way ahead of her, muttering to himself as he made his preparations.

"Ah the scene of my great defeat – curse that boy and his meddling! I'll make him pay alright. And that pretty young daughter of his too – oh she'll pay for the pair of them when I'm done, oh yes…"

At that moment the dark mage turned. "Ah good, I see you've joined us at last. I was just considering how best I might make you suffer once we're done."

Phae's temper rose. "I heard what you were saying mage. He'll come for you. He'll destroy you just as he did last time. I know who you are… Varrus!"

Varrus smirked with delight. "My-oh-my we are a clever one, aren't we? Can't have gained that from your father's side that's for sure! Come to think of it, who *is* your mother?"

Phae locked her mouth tightly shut. She wouldn't tell him for all the pain in the world. It might just be the one thing that could save her.

Varrus shrugged and extended his hand towards her. Once more his voice took on that same alluring tone that had so easily deceived her when they first met. She struggled to resist. "Come my child, don't you worry about telling me just yet. There will be plenty of time for talking later; right now, I need you to do something for me. I need you to remember the spell I taught you at the Lake."

Phae's body went stiff. She could feel the powers building within her. The magic was not of her own making. Again, she was completely helpless.

The voice of the dark mage entered her mind.

"Well done child, I see you've remembered my spell perfectly. This second source should be as nothing to a mage as powerful as you. You should consider yourself privileged. No ordinary mortal should have access to the power of the gods. You find yourself, in a most privileged position."

Phae gulped. She did her best to ignore the mage and instead focus on not being sick. Since they had closed the first source her headaches had certainly been better – most likely something of the mage's doing – but now, here at the second source, they returned with a vengeance. Nausea swept through her body. She swallowed back the rising sickness in her stomach.

"That's it my child. Only a little more now."

In front of her Phae saw a ring of stone set in the ground. From her father's stories she knew this must have been the place her father had first foiled Varrus' plans to destroy the realm of men.

And here she was, daughter of two of the heroes of the realm, undoing all the good they had done in years past; undoing the realm itself.

The weight of history and the burden of her unwilling task hung heavy on her shoulders. She could sense the dark mage's delight as the second source began to rise up out of the ground.

"Yes… good…"

As before, she set to work manipulating the glowing colour sphere in strange contorted patterns. The world itself seemed to bend around her hands.

And then… nothing.

As her spell reached its climax the source faded and shrunk to a size no bigger than her fist. She wanted to weep, but her tears had dried up many weeks before. Instead she retched violently as the dark mage's presence left her and her stomach decided it had seen enough.

There was little more the dark mage could do now to make her feel any worse than she did. All she could do was close her eyes and pray that the pain would go away. She didn't have long before her prayers were answered.

9

The weeks passed slowly. With each day Phae slipped further from their grasp. They travelled further than they'd ever travelled together as a group before – from the first rays of dawn through each day and then well into the night. Fortune favoured them slightly at least – on their journey south they made a brief detour back to Keln where Callum borrowed a cart and a pair of horses from the generous village folk. But however hard they pushed, and however far they travelled, Phae still seemed to be slipping away. Her trail was now almost impossible to follow, and with each passing day Aaron found his task that much harder than the day before.

They barely spoke as they travelled – each member of the party lost in his or her own thoughts as high above them a black spot stained the sky, masking a small part of the sun. They made camp that night just as they always did; Callum wandered off in search of firewood while Aaron arranged their meal and Lena tended to their horses. All of a sudden, Lena let out a yelp. Aaron turned. "Are you alright?"

Lena held her fingers to her temples and contorted her face. "My head…"

Aaron shifted over to where she sat. "Are you ill?"

"I don't… I…"

Just then Callum staggered back to the campsite. Firewood clattered to the ground as he fell to his knees, his head in his hands.

"Argh!"

"Callum?" Aaron looked around helplessly, unsure as to what he was supposed to do. "What's wrong?" he stammered. Beside him, Lena grasped his hand. She squeezed so hard he let out a small cry. "Not so hard Lena I–"

His words were cut off. Callum grabbed his water bottle and took a deep swig. "Magic," he gasped. "The source…"

"But the second source is miles away! It's in the far south, it's…"

Callum nodded slowly. "I know."

Just then, their pain started to fade. Aaron let out a sigh as Lena released his hand and his two friends slowly returned to their normal selves. As the pain subsided, Callum collected the scattered firewood and brought it over to the fire.

As soon as the flame was built sufficiently they prepared their meal in silence as they each gathered their thoughts.

Aaron was the first to speak. "I think we all know what this means."

Lena's voice was barely a whisper. "She's closed another source…" She looked to Callum. "She can't be doing this on her *own*, can she?"

Callum stared silently at the flames for a moment before turning to face her. His voice was choked, "I don't know," he whispered. "I just don't know what to think anymore. All this time I've been hoping to find her the victim of some evil plot against us, but every day we follow the trail and see just the one set of hoof-prints I can't help but think it might not be the case. She's a clever girl – and powerful too. She's suffering, and she's desperate. Given all that's happened I just don't know what to think. She's capable of just about anything."

Lena paused as she composed herself. Her voice was remarkably calm. "I don't think," she said, "we should concern ourselves yet with what might or what might not be. I've not come all this way to see my dearest friends suffer, and I certainly haven't come all this way to see them lose hope. If there's anything I've learnt over the years it's to trust in hope. Together we can always overcome whatever trials may face us. We need to be strong for each other now – we must be strong for Phae. First thing's first we need to find her and stop her causing any more harm. After that, we need to see about repairing the sources and restoring magic to the realm." She looked sternly at her two companions. "Are there any questions?"

There was silence.

Slowly, Callum nodded.

They rose early the next morning. As soon as he rose from his slumber Aaron was able to confirm what they all feared: the second source had closed and his sight was failing rapidly. Only Lena was able to offer them any crumb of hope.

"I've been thinking," she said.

"Oh?"

"If you think about it," Lena continued, "so far everything Phae has done has been to a pattern, to a purpose. She headed for the Lake – one of the known sources of magic in this realm – and as we all know, she somehow managed to close it. After that she headed south and as we have now confirmed, has managed to close the next source."

Callum frowned. "Stupid question I know, but just how many sources of magic are there?" he asked. "I'm certainly not as well read on the subject as you are, but as far as I can recall there are three recorded sites where researchers have proposed there to be sources: Lake Forever, the ancient Va'leri Monoliths and…"

"Stormy Falls," Lena nodded her head.

It was now Aaron's turn to frown. "Are they where I think they are?"

"The north east, yes."

"You don't think she'll really be heading there next do you?"

"Well it would certainly make sense," Lena replied. "And so given how far behind her we are already, there's a good chance if we head east we can cut her off on her journey back north. At the very least we can close on her trail."

Callum rubbed his chin. "Well it's certainly a risk," he said slowly. "But then what you're saying makes a lot of sense. She's already way ahead of us and pulling away with each passing day. If we can cut off the bottom point of the triangle we may well start to catch her."

"But what if she continues further south?" Aaron asked. "If she continues south out of the realm we might never catch her."

Callum sighed. "Well if she does that my friend then I fear we may well have far greater challenges to worry about. If we can't find a way to restore the sources soon the whole realm could descend into chaos." He took a deep breath. "Lena's right," he said. "We need to catch her, but we also need to think about the bigger picture. If she *is* heading for the third and – as far as we know – final source, then we need to get there as quickly as we can. If she succeeds in closing it then I dread to think what might happen. A realm without magic is a terrifying thought. If she shuts the source then everything the Seer predicted might come true – and perhaps worse things still." He took another deep breath and looked at each of his companions in turn. "It's decided," he said at last, "we head east."

10

Through the long dark of the abyss, the voice of the star-god rushed into the dark emissary's mind.

"It is time Varrus."

"Time for what my Lord?"

"It is time for you to pave the way for my release; time for you to begin to reap the rewards of your loyal service to me."

Varrus felt a surge of power rush through him. Sparks flickered between his fingertips. He could feel the magic inside him begin to grow. But it wasn't a magic of the mortal realm – it was a magic far more captivating than that: it was the magic of the void.

Varrus sucked in a deep breath.

"Savour this moment my servant. Become one with the magic I have given you. The final tasks will require every ounce of your being as I ready my escape."

Varrus quivered with excitement. "What would you have me do my Lord?"

The star-god paused a moment. Varrus waited in eager anticipation for the star-god's final commands.

"Prepare for battle my servant," the booming voice said at last. *"Sow fear among the people of this land. Though my power grows by the day there are yet those in this pitiful realm who will try and stop me. You must destroy them. The heart of the foul magic that pervades this world finds many ways to break through to the mortal plain. The three ancient sources are not the only wells of power in this realm. Close them Varrus, and freedom will be mine at last!"*

With these words the star-god left Varrus' mind and he was left free once more to act of his own accord. He turned towards the slumbering form of the girl. With the power of the gods on his side he might finally break her defences and put her to more use yet…

Phae's eyes snapped open.

Or did they?

As usual she found the dark mage leering over her. Whether sleeping or no, the foul fetid stench of the mage's breath made her retch. The mage took a step back.

"Ah so I see you are awake at last. My enchantments are clearly losing their strength…"

"What do you want *mage*?" Phae spat petulantly at her captor's feet. "What evil would you have me do now? Have you not had your fill already?"

"Oh, I could never have my fill of evil my dear," Varrus grinned wickedly, "for it's in my blood you see. And in yours too it would seem."

Phae went stiff as a strange tingling sensation ran through her body.

"What have you done to me?" she demanded, "What cruel trick is this you're using on me now?"

"Ah just you wait and see my girl," Varrus replied. "You see it all has to do with your father."

"My father? What has my father got to do with this?"

"Wouldn't *you* like to know," Varrus hissed. "Usually I wouldn't divulge such information to one such as you, but in this particular case I might make an exception. While up to now I have done my best to conceal you from him and avoid capture it seems my plans now require me to attract his attention."

"His *attention*?! You must be crazy. He'll kill you when he finds out what you've done to me!"

"Ah yes and there rests the crux of the plan," Varrus continued. "For though he would sorely love to kill me for a second time, with you as my hostage he will be powerless to stop me. I will strike when my enemy is at his weakest, and so will achieve my finest victory!

He smiled wickedly at her. "It is my girl, as you will no doubt appreciate, a very cunning plan."

"He'll never let you get away with this!" Phae shrieked, "*I'll* never let you get away with this! Try as you may Varrus I will fight you every step of the way!"

The dark mage sighed and shook his head. "And here I was thinking thought of your father might prove incentive to you," he said. "It seems I must resort to more – how shall we say – 'brutal' means of achieving your compliance after all..."

Phae screamed. A few moments later, her mind went blank.

She woke she knew not how many hours or even days later, to find the dark mage not leering over her as he was so often want to do, but instead peering ahead into the distance. The length of rope that bound her waist was clutched tightly in his grip.

She followed the direction of his gaze. There, no more than a mile or so from where they stopped, a small village sat atop the crest of a large hill. "This I suppose will be as good a place to start as any," he said finally, turning to examine his prisoner. "Come along my girl – there's killing to be done."

Phae resisted as best she could but the dark mage was too strong. In a matter of moments, the mage was looking her directly in the eye. "Now my child," he said slowly, "now you must search deep within yourself for that fountain of power your parents knew nothing about. Open yourself to the spring of magic coursing within you. Take it my child – take it and mould it. Seize it my child, for today we will reap our revenge upon the old world!"

Phae tried to scream, but no sound left her mouth. The mage had already seen fit to steal her body, and now he had stolen her voice as well.

He will not have my soul!

She struggled every step of the way as Varrus dragged her along towards the village, screaming into *his* mind even if she couldn't scream out into the physical world. She could feel him inside her, laughing at her helpless struggles, savouring in the power he seemed to be drawing from her.

As they approached the village they caught sight of a young man hard at work gathering his crop. He looked up as the first bolts of lightning shot out from the dark mage's hands.

The young farmer died without a sound.

Another villager stepped out from behind an outbuilding. She too died in an instant.

"Now girl: your turn."

Phae felt the presence of Varrus inside her, manipulating her magics to build a fiery hailstorm for the villagers gathered round the southernmost building. Though she could not stop him directly, she fought through gritted teeth to send the attack off course.

The fiery comets missed the villagers by a few feet and instead caught the building they were standing by and sent it up in flame. The villagers ran for cover, screaming and shouting at their loved ones to escape. Men with buckets ran for the burning building, but even as they did so, more of the dark mage's cruel lightning struck them down.

It was a massacre. The villagers were helpless against them.

Varrus cackled wildly as the fire spread and more souls were caught by his deadly bolts. After Phae's first thwarted attack he decided to ignore her and attack solely on his own. Phae was grateful for this one small mercy.

In a matter of minutes, the village was no more. Tears streamed down young Phae's cheeks.

"Stop your whingeing girl," Varrus scolded. He pointed to the blazing village. "If that doesn't get your father's attention, I don't know what will!"

* * *

Callum stared into the distance through tired, half-closed eyes. He hadn't slept properly for weeks and as their cart trundled tediously on its way he would find his head sagging forward and his eyes threatening to close. But each time they did so, a bump or a jolt would snap him awake and so the cycle would continue. The cold certainly didn't help matters either.

Why was it so cold in the middle of summer?

He raised his head and stared long and hard at the dark blotch that continued to grow in the sky. It was almost like it was sucking up the energy of the world itself the weather was so strange. He couldn't help but think this all had something to do with Phae...

In the back of the cart, Aaron dozed fitfully.

Seated beside him, Lena too stared at the sky.

Callum shivered as a particularly biting wind swept across the valley they were driving through. Lena reached behind her and produced a blanket. She put it round him.

"You really should try and get some rest you know," she said gently. "It'll do no one any good when we finally find out whatever's going on and you're too tired to act."

Callum raised a faint smile. If it wasn't for his two friends he didn't know what he'd do right now. As much as he felt compelled to stay awake and offer Lena what little company he could, with the blanket wrapped tightly around him, he felt himself drifting off to sleep.

He slept for the rest of the day and most of the night as well, until Aaron finally shook him awake for his turn on watch. He rubbed his eyes tiredly as they adjusted to the dark of the night.

He looked over to where Lena lay curled up beside a small fire his companions must have lit while he was still asleep. Callum clicked his fingers absently as he considered their situation. Their morale was at rock bottom, but since they had changed their course at least they felt like they had a purpose – that they were taking an active step to try and alter their fate. Despite his fading sight and her failing magics, both Aaron and Lena had been stalwart in their resolve to continue on to whatever end their path might lead them to. Together they could conquer any enemy; defeat any challenge. The problem they faced however, was working out *how*.

He looked up to the sky as he continued to absently click his fingers.

It was an annoying habit he had developed over the past few months, but since he had started to study the powers of the elements more closely of late, it was one he just couldn't shake. Sparks crackled between his fingers as he did so.

Sparks…

Callum considered waking the others, but thought better of it. He sat in silence as he stared at his hands.

11

The morning came, and with it a brief respite from the biting cold that had swept over them in the night. Callum was sure it was getting colder – just as he was sure the blotch covering the sun was getting bigger – but right now all he could think about were the sparks he was creating between his fingers.

Lena watched with fascination as he absently clicked his fingers while they prepared breakfast. Since the second source had closed she hadn't even the slightest trace of water-magic at her disposal.

Finally, Callum stopped what he was doing and looked up to meet her gaze. Silent communion passed between them.

"So, what do you think?" he asked.

Lena frowned. "I don't know. I mean they certainly appear to be sparks of magic but just why you have access to them while the rest of us don't..."

"But that's the thing: I *don't* have access to my powers – or at least I don't think I do. I feel... different somehow, but I just can't figure out what it is inside me that's causing the magic to flow." To prove a point, he moved his two index fingers together and with a snap, a particularly large bolt flashed between them. He sat back and shrugged. "I haven't got a clue."

"No change there then," Aaron jested from across the camp. "You know Callum instead of clicking your fingers you could be doing something useful about now, like say, helping me with this."

Callum looked over to where his friend was struggling to prepare breakfast. Now Aaron's magical sight was fading, even simple tasks were becoming a bother. Callum scolded himself silently.

"Sorry, you're right," he said as he passed Aaron their small cooking pan. "I've been so caught up in my own problems I really should have thought more about the rest of you."

"Well I can't exactly blame you," Aaron replied, "but a little less of the whole 'self-absorbed melancholy Callum' would be nice."

"You're right," Callum said with a nod, "I'm sorry. This journey's been tough for *all* of us – I should remember that. I really am grateful for you coming with me I–"

"Oh, enough of that," Aaron cut him off sharply. "I get the picture. You'd have done the same for us if the situation were reversed."

Lena nodded. "Aaron's right – you don't need to thank us Callum. That's what friends are for."

They finished breakfast quickly, and were soon underway. They continued to follow the path east for another two days before it branched and they followed a road that wound its way towards the north. A few days later and they came upon a large market town in which they were able to buy more provisions. It was as Aaron was paying for their goods that they heard the first whisperings of trouble.

Instinctively, Aaron pressed the shopkeeper for more information.

"Well sir, far be it for me to speculate on a tale of such ill tidings, but word is a plague of death is spreading across the north. Some say it's the wrath of the gods. Trade has all but dried up since the first tidings reached us!"

"What do you mean 'wrath of the gods'?" Aaron interrupted. "What exactly has been happening?"

"Fires sir. Death and destruction!" The shopkeeper cast a wary glance towards Lena who stood a few paces behind him, alongside Callum. "Some of the things I've heard are not the sorts to be uttered in the presence of a lady, but I can tell you for a fact it's not pleasant. Why my young son who was on an errand for me said he could smell the stench of death from over a mile away!"

Aaron frowned. "I don't suppose you could mark on my map for me where these villages are could you?"

"My heavens!" the shopkeeper was startled. "I wouldn't advise going anywhere near them sir if I were you. There's nothing but bad omens coming from those villages. Certainly no place for a lady! I'd keep well away if I were you sir."

"Well, just for interest's sake then," Aaron replied, "At least then we know where to avoid."

The shopkeeper looked dubious, but after a bit more persuasion marked the sites of the three fire-struck villages he knew of. Aaron thanked him and turned on his way. His face was grim. Ahead of him he Callum and Lena were already heading for the door.

"I take it you all heard that?"

They both nodded.

"Right then, let's be on our way shall we."

The first village was less than a day's ride from the town, and they reached it early the following morning.

Though the rumours had told them to expect the worst, none of them were quite prepared for the scene that would confront them. The dead were everywhere, scattered in their panic to escape the flames. But it wasn't the fire that had killed them; it was something else. Callum coughed as he fought back the foul stench of death. Beside him, Lena's words echoed his thoughts. "It's just like Keln," she said softly.

Callum cast his eyes across the desecrated remains of the village. Lena was right: it *was* just like Keln – but it was different too. In Keln, one of Varrus' cadre of powerful mages had slaughtered the inhabitants to absorb their life force. However evil and contrived the reasoning, at least in some twisted way it had meaning, but *this*… this was just slaughter.

Lena shook her head sadly. "Poor, poor people."

Aaron put his arm around her.

Callum stood just apart from them. He could taste something on the air; something beyond the stench of death and decay. He could sense… magic. He closed his eyes and tried to recall some of the power that seemed lost to him. It was like the trace in the air was calling to him somehow. It seemed familiar…

He clicked his fingers absently as he concentrated.

There, faint as anything, he could taste the familiar trace of someone, the very thought of whom made his blood run cold.

The word was but a whisper on his lips.

"Varrus."

Aaron and Lena gasped as one.

"But I thought he was dead?" said Aaron.

"Not dead: just 'disappeared'," Lena replied. "Callum defeated him remember."

Callum nodded. "I'd know his scent anywhere."

"But if Varrus has come back to the old world then that means…"

Aaron squeezed her tighter to him. "We all know what that means," he said softly. "It means the world is in far graver danger than we could ever have imagined."

"And Phae…" Lena stammered.

"And Phae." Aaron nodded.

Callum took a deep breath. Anger coursed through his veins. And yet at the same time he was filled with strength.

They had purpose.

"I think," he said at last, "I think it's time we moved out. We've waited long enough here. The longer we tarry the more people will die to Varrus' schemes, and the more danger for poor Phae."

He walked back to the cart. "We don't have a moment to lose."

12

In the strange land of her half-sleep, Phae screamed.

All around her buildings burnt and people died at the hands of the dark mage's magic – *her* magic – that had caused so much death and destruction already. She couldn't help but think of poor Master Kulgrim and the cruel fate he had suffered because of what she had done.

Because of her...

Their trail of destruction had lasted for weeks now. Weeks and weeks of needless slaughter.

Once word had started to spread through the region, some of the towns and villages they encountered were prepared – and some even had a small garrison ready to meet them at the gates. No matter how hard they tried, they all met the same fate.

And she was powerless to stop him.

He had full control now, her indomitable will eventually sapped by endless days of struggle against the mage's dark magics that kept her trapped in a perpetual state of half-sleep. She had nothing left now to combat his evil spells save the hope that someone somewhere was looking for her.

She clutched the picture of her parents tightly in her hand. It was all she had left...

Up ahead of her the dark mage cackled in delight as his short-lived pleasure came to an end and the last of the villagers died.

He tugged on the rope that still bound her to him. He caught her as she approached.

"Well my girl I can't see your cursed father ignoring *this*," he said, casting his arm towards the desecrated village. "With every town and village that dies so my strength increases and so his must wane. Only one more source to go, and then his beloved island of wizards must fall.

"But I get ahead of myself," the mage said reflectively. "The night is still young and if we're lucky we may yet reach the next town before I must let myself rest. Come," he said, placing his arm around her shoulders. "It's time we continued our dark crusade."

He cackled again.

Before Phae had a chance to even think about crying, again her world went blank.

* * *

They were closing on the trail. It was only a matter of time now. Callum sat at the front of the cart, Aaron squeezed in beside him while Lena sat in the back huddled under a large blanket. He clicked his fingers absently as he stared fixedly into the distance. For some reason there was an intuitive magic still at work inside him, and while Lena's magics had all but faded completely, along with a large portion of Aaron's sight, *he* still had powers of sorts. It was just a matter of working out how on earth he was supposed to use them…

He turned in his seat to check on Lena. She shot him a smile. He was just about to say something when his thoughts were distracted by a prod in his side.

"You know Callum I've been thinking…"

"Oh no, here we go," Lena sighed. Aaron chose to ignore her.

"So, as I say I've been thinking," he continued. "If Varrus is back from the dead and is using magic to destroy villages, where on earth is he getting his magic from? I mean far be it for me to comment on such things but given Lena and I are but shadows of our former selves and the best you can muster is a small spark between your fingers, just where is Varrus getting his magic from?"

Callum turned his gaze towards the heavens. The blotch that had at first been only the merest blemish in the summer sky was now almost as big as his outstretched hand. Even looking at the ominous eclipse sent a shiver down his spine.

He turned in his seat. "What do you think Lena?" he asked.

Lena shook her head. "I just don't know…"

Callum sighed. He wished Kiera was with them. She'd know what to do. She always did.

Slowly the miles passed them by…

* * *

Varrus sucked in a deep, rasping breath as behind him his unconscious charge drifted silently in her magically-induced sleep.

Though her face was serene he knew inside that pretty little head of hers a war was raging. She had been nothing but trouble since the moment he had set eyes on her.

He would soon make her pay; he would soon make *all* of them pay.

He looked ahead to where the dark shape of Stormy Falls loomed large in the distance. Named for its frothing, tempestuous rapids and its miles of sharp rocks, Varrus really could think of no better place for his final victory over the girl and her cursed father.

A slow lingering death was the least Callum deserved.

The trap was set, the bait ready; now all he had to do was wait.

13

Phae's eyes snapped open. Something was wrong – very wrong. She struggled against the bonds of magic that held her in place.

"There, there, little one, don't be afraid," Varrus called over to her from the bank. "I wouldn't look down if I were you."

Phae did look down. She was suspended over the precipice is a massive waterfall. The waterfall was so high she couldn't even see the bottom through the spray. One thing was for certain: a single command from the dark mage and her life would come to an end.

She closed her eyes and began to pray.

"Oh, prayers won't help you my child," Varrus scoffed. "After all I have the gods on my side, look."

Phae tried her best to ignore him but as she turned her head away visions of her father's face flashed inside her mind. A thin, cruel smile formed on Varrus' lips. "Oh, I haven't done anything to him… yet," he said at last. He paused as he savoured in Phae's torture. "But he'll be here soon I can assure you of that!"

Phae's expression changed. "He's really coming?"

"Oh yes he's coming alright – and he's bringing those annoying friends of his too."

"Aaron… Lena…"

The dark mage nodded tersely. Phae could tell he grew weary of the conversation. Her hands started to tremble as she felt the dark mage's mind slipping into hers. His voice echoed inside her head.

"Have no fear my pretty, your father will be here soon enough. But before he is, you and I have a lot of work to do."

In the recesses of her mind Phae cried out, as once more the dark mage took control.

* * *

Callum looked to the sky as far above them dark clouds gathered and the heavens opened.

It was no ordinary rain.

Lena suggested the name Stormy Falls was much more than a name – that there was magic to the place that gave it its title. Judging by the weight and ferocity of the storm, Callum was inclined to agree.

She sat beside him, rubbing her arms with her hands to try and generate some heat. As he caught her eye, he realised that she wasn't cold at all: she was just as nervous as he was.

They had spent weeks on the road and now it seemed the end was in sight.

The cart jolted on the hard ground. Behind him Aaron moaned as pools of water splashed over his legs.

All around them the wind was picking up, sending rain in all directions. Callum wiped his eyes with his sleeve. He had to raise his voice just to be heard over the growing storm. "Can you see anything Lena?"

"I can barely see a thing!" she shouted in reply. Just then she raised a hand. "Wait, I hear water!"

"Now's really not the time for joking Lena," Aaron called out from behind them. "I may be nigh-on blind, but I am not *stupid*!"

As if to make his point, lightning crackled overhead and a gust of wind soaked him in spray. His expression was less than amused. "It's pretty darn wet back here already I think you'll find!"

"No, you don't understand – I hear *running* water. I can hear the sound of water breaking on rocks. We must be close!" Lena shouted. She turned to Callum. "What do we do?"

He gritted his teeth. "We do only what we can do," he said firmly. "We continue to follow the path."

Lena was about to say something but her words were drowned out by thunder. Their horses started to whine nervously. She jumped down from the cart and moved to calm them. "I think I'd better lead them by foot from here on in," she called out to her companions. "There's no way they'll make it up the steep rise otherwise."

Callum nodded. For all the talk of crashing water in the distance he was sure he could taste magic on the air.

The storm continued to rage around them as they led their cart up the steep ascent. All around them, thick, weather-beaten trees clung to the hard ground wherever they could. In more than one place fallen trunks crossed their path and they had to carefully navigate around them in what were by now treacherous conditions.

Callum wiped his face with his sleeve. Streams of water ran down his face and dropped from his nose and his brow. He peered into the gloom.

"See anything Callum?"

"No, not yet," he replied. He paused. "So much for summer eh?"

Behind him, Aaron laughed. "Well you certainly saved that one up didn't you!" Even Callum was forced to grin at his friend's remark. "I know you could do with a wash Callum but this is getting ridiculous!"

Callum was about to respond when all of a sudden Lena called them to a halt.

"I see a light."

"A light?"

"Yes, a light up ahead – look."

Lena pointed into the gloom and Callum followed her gaze, squinting hard through the rain. Sure enough, there in the distance the faintest of lights shone out through the dark.

They led the horses only a little further on up the track, and left them in the best shelter they could find. Aaron meanwhile searched the back of the cart for his sword and made sure it was attached firmly to his belt.

"Well I don't know how much use it will be to me," he said, "but at least it's something."

Callum nodded. It had been hard for Aaron, coming to terms with his loss of sight, but stoic as ever, he made do as best he could.

As soon as the cart was secured they continued to edge their way into the gloom. Despite ridding themselves of their encumbrance, the going soon became even more treacherous as the gradient increased and strong winds buffeted them from all sides. More than a dozen times Callum felt his feet slipping beneath him, and he cursed his luck repeatedly as each time he slipped he was covered in mud. His entire body ached with the strain of the ascent, though for all his troubles, Aaron's were ten times worse. He turned and took hold of his friend's left arm as Lena already had hold of his right. Arm in arm, the three companions marched their way slowly up the hill. It took them what felt like hours to reach the top of the rise where the ground finally levelled out and they set eyes upon the bank of rocks that helped give the 'Falls their name.

The noise was like nothing else. Water crashed on rocks and frothed and swirled in a tempest the likes of which they had never seen. Even a dozen paces from the bank the spray was awesome and soaked them even more than the pelting rain.

At Aaron's side, Lena was shaking like a leaf. The raging torrent was stirring something inside her. Callum changed his position in their chain and moved to Lena's right-hand side. He squeezed her arm reassuringly. They would get through this together. Whatever Varrus had to throw at them, they would be ready.

The light was getting closer...

They carried on, one step at a time, slowly heading towards the light. The closer they got, the louder the sound of the rapids beside them and the greater the spray washed up in their faces.

Callum did his best to ignore it. He focussed solely on the light ahead. He was sure if he strained hard enough he could just make out the shape of a figure.

Was he dreaming?

They quickened their pace. With every step the shape drew into clearer focus.

"Phae is that you?" Callum let go of Lena's arm and dashed forwards. "Phae?"

She floated, suspended on a cushion of air above the precipice of the waterfall, torrential spray showering her as the rapids hit the sharp rocks far below. Somehow, she remained dry. Her voice was distant and faded. "Father... *He*'s inside me... help me!"

Callum felt his heart skip a beat. His little girl was in danger. As his eyes adjusted to the bright light of her being he saw at last the spell she was weaving. The power was fantastic. Though her hands manipulated the magic with practiced skill, he knew the movements were not her own.

Callum could feel the hairs on the back of his neck start to rise. Not only was his little girl in danger, but his ancient foe was waiting for him somewhere out there in the storm. And worse than that, he was powerless to do anything about it. He just couldn't gain access to his magic.

It was Aaron who made the first move. "Varrus!" he yelled, "Come out and face us!"

From the shadows of the opposite bank, the dark mage stepped forward. Phae's glow cast him in an intimidating light. He was... *changed* somehow. Though he still looked the same as he had way back when the three companions had encountered him last, the power he exercised seemed foreign and strange. He waved to them from across the river. In one of the most chilling scenes Callum had ever witnessed, the dark mage's voice began to project from his daughter's lips.

"It's been a long time, *boy*. You're looking well I see."

"What have you done to my daughter Varrus?" Callum shouted across the river. "What foul scheme is this?"

"No need to shout, *boy*," the voice of Varrus (through Phae) replied, "I can hear you perfectly well enough. Such a fragile creature this daughter of yours – and such a beauty too. If only you knew the potential within her! But alas you won't be around much longer to see our final union. You see, other than bringing you here to let you witness my ultimate victory, I also brought you here to *die*! I do hope you enjoy your last moments with your daughter. Children can be such a pain sometimes..."

With these words an explosion knocked the three companions to the ground. By the time they regained their footing, Phae was upon them.

* * *

Anger coursed through Phae's veins.

She'd never known such a feeling of hatred and wrath in all her tender years, but right now, it threatened to consume her.

It was the dark mage's doing – she knew that much. On the far bank Varrus stood and watched proceedings with unnatural delight.

All of a sudden, an explosion rocked her and sent her father and his friends tumbling to the ground. As they recovered she could feel the yet unfinished spell start to slip away from her. She watched helplessly as Varrus drew the source towards him.

"*It's alright girl, I'll finish with the spell. My powers are such that I can complete what you started for me...*" He took the source in his hands and started to work on the magical strands. "*It's time you reacquainted yourself with your father.*"

Phae screamed but no words left her lips. She was trapped. The mage controlled her completely.

Helpless, she drifted towards the shore...

* * *

Callum hit the floor and rolled to the side. Beside him Aaron and Lena both had the wind knocked out of them. If it hadn't been for his quick reactions they would all have been hit by the wave of fire Phae had sent hurtling towards them. He helped his companions to their feet.

Floating high above them, the fragile wraith-like form of Phae cackled wickedly. The voice of Varrus echoed from her lips. "Like that did you boy? There's more where that came from you know!"

Another wave of fire flew from Phae's outstretched hands. In days gone by Callum or Lena might have been able to raise a shield to protect them, but now with the last source of magic fading, they were helpless against the onslaught. It was as if she drew power directly from the source itself.

They dived to the ground again as the second wave of fire threatened to engulf them.

Aaron swore as he hit the ground hard. A large gash opened up on the side of his face. "Callum, what do we do?"

He shook his head wearily. "I don't know…"

Suddenly, the voice from up above them changed. "Can't… fight him. You must… help me."

Phae's face was contoured in agony. High above them, she struggled for control. "I can't stop… the attacks…" As she said this, balls of fire shot out from her hands – burning comets alive with fierce crackling energy. At the last moment she tried to turn them away from their targets. "I'm sorry…"

"Run!"

Callum grabbed Aaron and dragged him down the slope while Lena ran in the opposite direction.

Varrus' voice again cackled over the tumult of the crashing waters beside them. "You can run boy but you can't hide!"

As he said this the fiery comets turned once more and started to gather on Callum's position. Lena at least was safe, but could do nothing but watch in horror as Callum and Aaron ran for their lives.

Callum pushed his friend away from him. "Run Aaron! Let them take me! Escape while you can!"

Aaron tried to resist but as his friend released him he found he was lost with no one to guide him. He tentatively made to move away from the sound of Callum's voice.

From up above, Phae watched helplessly as the magics of her own making gathered upon her father. She couldn't stop them. The magic was just too strong.

Callum turned just as the searing heat of the comets told him there was no escape. He stopped and opened his arms to confront his doom head on. "Do your worst Varrus!" he yelled. "You may kill me but rest assured there will be others. You *will* be stopped!"

The fireballs circled around him.

Lena rushed forwards. "Callum!"

She was too late.

At Varrus' command, the fiery spheres crashed into Callum's being, engulfing him in flame.

"No!"

High above them, Phae screamed. "Father!" She struggled fiercely against her bonds. Already she could feel her magic fading as the final source neared closure. The voice of the dark mage cackled inside her head.

"Not long to go now my pretty."

"You will die for what you've done mage!"

"Oh?"

A voice both familiar and reassuring rose from the bank. "Don't give up Phae." Instinctively, Phae turned towards the shore. From the smouldering remains of the fire, her father stepped forward, his eyes burning a deep crimson red.

"No, this cannot be!" Varrus cursed. "You're supposed to be dead!"

"I could say the same about you," Callum replied, standing together once more with his two dearest friends. "We've defeated you once Varrus; we'll defeat you again."

"Ah, but can you defeat your own daughter? That is the question."

As these words issued forth from Phae's lips, her hand reached down to her belt. Unbeknownst to her, the mage had supplied her with a dagger during her last enchanted sleep. She struggled against the compulsion, but the power was too great to resist. Her hand rested on the hilt. She drew it from its sheath and brandished the blade before her.

The three companions gasped as Phae floated down towards them. She hovered just a few feet above the ground.

Slowly but surely, she advanced on Callum.

Lena held her hand to her mouth, her eyes wide with fear. "No…" she gasped.

"No Phae, don't do it." Aaron drew his sword and moved to block her path. His sight may have faded but he was still as brave as ever.

Callum pushed his friend aside and stepped forward. Phae stared at him. Their eyes met.

"Fight it Phae, don't let the dark mage win."

Tears streamed down her face.

Despite the advancing blade, Callum stood firm. His eyes never left hers. "Fight him Phae. Fight him with all your heart–"

"I… can't…" she sobbed. "He's so strong, he–"

Her blade was now only a matter of inches from Callum's chest. She was so close but she just couldn't pull away. She couldn't…

Then she felt it. Her one and only chance. For one brief moment his powers were stretched. As the source was near closure she had but one chance to resist the dark mage's control.

She closed her eyes and concentrated for all she was worth. Above them, the sky rumbled as the storm grew in intensity.

"I'm sorry," she said softly, as with one last concerted burst of energy, she flung herself into the air.

Varrus cursed as she fought against him, but such was the burden of his current task he couldn't bring his full power to bear. In that instant Phae did the only thing she could: she pushed herself to the furthest limits of her magical chain, hovering over the dark abyss of the Stormy Falls, her life hanging on a tender thread.

No power in the universe would make her do that which the dark mage had commanded her. She'd caused enough pain already.

She sobbed bitterly as she watched the final source close. As it did, she felt the last of her powers ebb and the spell holding her in a permanent dream-state come to an end.

With it came to an end the magics suspending her in the air above the 'Falls.

She bid farewell to those who had fought so hard to save her. "Goodbye my friends."

With these words, she plummeted to her doom.

"No!" Callum and Lena both rushed to the cliff edge. They could barely see even half-way to the bottom. Meanwhile the ground beneath their feet shook as the earth struggled to come to terms with the death of magic.

Lena held her head in her hands. Callum fell to his knees. Behind them both, as the blotch in the sky grew to cover the entire sun, Aaron stood alone and unmoving, his hands trembling at his side.

"My sight," he said softly, his words barely audible above the tumult of the rapids. "I'm blind."

Callum and Lena embraced each other tightly as the shock of events hit them. Phae was gone. There was nothing they could do. Callum looked up to the sky. "And so, the light of the world goes out…"

PART 2

THE DARKEST HOUR

1

Varrus screamed. In the blink of an eye his whole world was turned upside down and he found himself floating within the star-god's prison.

Skargyr's voice was a low rumble. *"Great shall be the reward for your loyalty my servant."*

Varrus gulped. Something was different. The star-god seemed to have grown in power since they had last met.

Varrus clutched the hilt of his sword to stop himself trembling. Adrenaline from his encounter with the boy and his friends still coursed through his veins. "What would you have me do next my Lord?"

The star-god paused, as if to take a deep breath. The sound was as thunder rumbling in the heavens. Varrus clutched his sword even tighter. His fingers started to lose feeling.

"As the magic of the old world fades so I am able to extend myself further beyond the bounds of my prison. While I yet draw my energy from the sun, still there are those who would try to stop me.

"Kill the mages Varrus. Destroy their kind so none may thwart me."

A cruel smile formed on Varrus' lips.

"Build me an army Varrus. Strike while the wizards are weak and their powers faded. Stop them raising a defence against my return."

"With great pleasure my Lord," Varrus replied. His hands no longer trembled as his mind was given to thoughts of reaping vengeance upon his former kin. Though he had failed to kill the boy thus far, he would take great pleasure in overseeing the boy's slow and lingering demise.

The star-god interrupted his thoughts. *"When the time comes my servant, you must be ready to receive me."*

Varrus bowed. "Of course, my Lord."

"Good," the star-god replied. Suddenly Varrus felt his body begin to shake. A wave of nausea swept over him, as once more he was sent spinning through the void...

Varrus opened his eyes and retched violently. The speed of transition between realms made his stomach clench and his legs shake beneath him. He caught himself with his hands as he fell to the ground, breathing deeply, taking in the enormity of the task his star-god master had set him. As soon as his stomach settled, he stood up and took a look at his new surroundings.

He had been transported to an island, somewhere in the middle of one of the distant oceans. He stood only a few dozen paces from the edge of a long sandy beach that stretched out for as far as he could see in either direction. The sand was still damp with the watermark of the high tide. A short distance away a teeming mass of shore-life was hard at work plundering the riches left behind by the departing sea.

There was something strange about this place – something pleasant even.

Varrus turned to face inland and stopped in fair amazement at the sight before him. There, amidst the thick foliage of a tropical forest, rose an enormous mountain so big it filled half the sky. Even from this far out Varrus could tell the mountain before him was far bigger than anything found in the realm of men, and dwarfed even the Dragontooth Mountains in the north. Craning his neck, he could just make out a trail of smoke rising from its tip. It was then he realised it wasn't just any mountain his dark lord had sent him to: it was a *volcano*.

It took him hours to cut his way through the thick forest to arrive at the volcano's base. As he reached the foot of the colossal fire-mountain he could understand why so many of his kind would make pilgrimages to the great mountains of the north. Compared to *those* mountains however, this single volcano was a *monster*, and the perfect location to raise an army in Skargyr's name.

As he stared up at the great mountain Varrus felt a tingle in his fingertips, the like of which he hadn't felt in quite some time. Not since before he had started to close the sources had he experienced a feeling such as this, and now, as he considered his options, he realised the true significance of the island the star-god had brought him to.

"Magic!" he exclaimed.

Varrus chuckled as he considered the genius of his master's plan. Why waste his own precious energy creating an army when he could feed off the magics of the world itself! "So, there is more magic left in the world after all..." he mused, as with a deep breath, he started to climb.

Hours passed. Eventually Varrus stopped to take his bearings. In the grand scheme of things, he had barely made a dent in terms of scaling the volcano's height, and yet he could sense his goal was close. With every step up the mountain he could feel the pull of magic getting stronger.

The familiar voice of the star-god boomed inside his head.

"A few more miles my servant, and you shall discover the power with which you are to build my armies."

Varrus nodded. He continued up the rocky mountainside as the star-god directed, following the tingle in his fingers that led him up and around the circumference until finally, he came upon a gap in the rock.

As he drew closer he could make out dark scorch marks in the mountainside and cracked chunks of volcanic rock scattered about the opening.

Varrus peered into the gloom of the dark passageway. His whole body trembled with excitement. The source of magic was close now, he could feel it; he could *taste* it.

A small bead of saliva formed at the corner of his mouth. He drew his sword and cast a simple illumination spell on its blade.

"Well, here it goes," he muttered, as he entered the heart of the mountain.

The passageway ran on for miles. For further that he could ever have imagined. Mile upon mile of scorched black rock marked his path and guided him on his way. The further he went, the hotter his path became as he neared the mountain's core.

After a short while Varrus paused to catch his breath. He was breathing hard and his robes were drenched with sweat. He desperately searched his memory for the words to a spell of cooling. As he did so, an involuntary impulse ran through him and the words of a spell unknown to him appeared on the tip of his tongue.

At once his body temperature cooled and his breathing slowed. Even now, in the depths of the world's greatest volcano, his master watched over him.

He felt the pull of the star-god's magic stronger than ever. Despite his weariness, he was pulled deeper into the heart of the mountain.

"Not far to go now my servant."

The pull of the star-god's magic became almost inexorable. Varrus wasn't even sure he still retained control of his legs.

"Yes, yes, deeper my servant. You must go deeper..."

Varrus closed his eyes and tried to think as he let the star-god's magic pull him on his way. What *did* Skargyr have planned for him? What was the star-god's real plan?

After some moments of consideration, his thoughts were broken as he realised he had reached his destination. A wave of relief hit him as the control of his bodily functions returned and he felt his legs at last come to a halt. He opened his eyes.

He stood now at the mountain's heart – a great molten pit of the earth's lifeblood stretched out as far as he could see. Way up in the very limits of Varrus' perception, a small dot of light marked the volcano's throat.

As he slowly regained control of his faculties he sensed at last the great weight of magic hanging heavy in the volcano's heart. It was almost as thick as the smoke that filled the air around him.

Varrus breathed deeply as the star-god spoke to him once more.

"I have brought you this far my servant, but now my powers in your realm grow weak. Build me an army Varrus. Build me an army with which I might reap vengeance upon the realm that holds the key to my eternal prison. Make me an army Varrus, and I shall grant you the greatest honour of all."

As the star-god's voice began to fade, Varrus felt the inclination to bow, though he wasn't even sure if his master could see him.

As soon as the voice had faded completely, he turned his attention at last upon the lava pit. It hissed and bubbled furiously as he approached it.

"Hmmm," Varrus mused, "where *is* the source?"

He stretched out his magical senses across the lake of lava in search of the focal point of the mountain's magic. The tides were strong, that was for certain. Powerful eddies tossed and turned him as he extended his magical self across the currents of the magical plain. As one stream came to an end, so he leapt to another, and then another, fighting hard to keep his focus and not succumb to the alluring flame. He gritted his teeth as he fought to keep his concentration.

Then he saw it.

Far out towards the centre of the lake the source of magic shone brightly amidst the burning pool. Its magical light illuminated the lava it rested in to an almost heavenly intensity. In that instant, Varrus knew why the star-god had chosen *this* as the place from which he would raise his army.

The volcanic source was the largest Varrus had ever seen. Its power far exceeded any he had seen thus far.

Varrus extended his senses forward and enveloped the source in his magical touch. As he devoted more and more of his magical self to the task of raising the source up from its molten cocoon, he felt himself grow in strength as the magics of the volcano gave him the energy he needed to continue.

As his power reached a crescendo, so his magics drew themselves beneath the fiery lake and grasped the source at once, pulling it eagerly to the surface where it shone to fill the entire cavern with a warm orange glow.

Varrus sheathed his sword as he drew the source to him. He could almost reach out and touch it, though he knew that to do so would be to touch creation itself.

He leaned out then, and gazed upon it a while. Even to him – one whose eyes were dim to such things – the source was a thing of unnatural beauty. He basked in its glow until finally he felt a tickling sensation within him prod him to return to the task at hand.

The star-god had left him with the knowledge with which to create his armies.

Varrus grinned wickedly.

Now the real fun would begin…

2

"And so the light of the world goes out," Lena whispered. Beside her, Callum knelt weeping at the cliff edge. Standing a short distance behind her, Aaron was numb with shock.

"My sight," he murmured, "it's gone."

Lena looked up to the heavens for some sign of hope but found none. Above them the thick black stain that covered the sun had grown to engulf the entire sun, casting their world in perpetual dusk. Not even she could find a glimmer of hope in this their darkest hour.

She took Aaron by the hand and gave it a squeeze. She had to be strong now – for all of them. Hers was the least burden to bear this dark day; the loss of her magic as nought compared to the loss of sight of he who was dearest to her, or the loss of a child, as Callum was now grieving.

All their efforts it seemed, had come to nothing.

And Varrus was gone.

On the far side of the rapids, there wasn't so much as a trace of the dark mage who had vanished the moment his task was complete. Lena knew there was more to this than met the eye, but right now, thought of Varrus and his evil schemes would have to wait.

She led Aaron gingerly over to where Callum knelt at the cliff's edge. With Phae gone and the world now cast in shadow, his grief consumed him. Weeks of bubbling emotions came to a head, and with all her heart, Lena prayed she would never again have to witness a sight as sorry as that before her. It was as if all hope had been completely washed away.

There was nothing she could say. Words failed her.

She said then, the only thing she could think to say. "We'd better go see to the horses."

Callum looked up. "What did you say?"

"I said we'd better go see to the horses," she said.

Somehow her words seemed to do the trick. After a long pause, Callum struggled to his feet. "That sounds like a good idea," he said.

Aaron meanwhile, remained silent and unmoving.

They made camp as best they could, though Lena found she had to do most of the work. Being perhaps the least able of the three in terms of field-craft, her attempts at making shelter were frustrated, but in the end, her efforts paid off.

Somehow – and she wasn't quite sure how – she managed to set up some cover beneath the thickest of trees she could find, and using the cart as one side of her construction, managed to make a small shelter as far out of the rain as she could manage with some sheets on the floor to keep off the mud.

As soon as she finished she guided Aaron over to the shelter first, and then cajoled Callum after him. As she finally sat down herself, just inside the edge of the shelter's protection, the rain stopped and the howling wind that had so hampered her came to an abrupt halt.

"Typical," she sighed. No one noticed her words. They were all still too overwhelmed with shock. She was almost tempted to cry herself looking at them, seeing them both so defeated in this way, but as grief threatened to overcome her, she grimaced and took a deep breath. She had to be strong now. She had to be strong for them all.

* * *

Callum woke with a jolt. As far as he could tell it was still the middle of the night, but given the twilight that had descended upon the world he couldn't be sure.

Beside him, in the close confines of their camp, his two companions slept. Aaron, his face pale and drawn with fatigue snored as he always did, his back resting against the cart. Next to him, Lena slept deeply, her head slumped forward over the pages of the small journal she carried wherever she went.

Callum wasn't sure how much time had passed since the fateful events at the 'Falls, but it felt like an age. He couldn't sleep anymore, that was for sure. His dreams were no longer a refuge from the troubles of the world. In fact, they were quite the opposite.

Over and over those last moments at the waterfall ran through his mind as he saw time and time again his only child falling helplessly to her doom.

And she hadn't so much as screamed.

It was as if she had *known* her course was the only one open to her and had accepted the consequences without so much as a second thought.

And she had so nearly killed him...

Callum thought back to the moment he had been engulfed in flame. Somehow – he still couldn't quite work out how – he had been spared from immolation. Had Phae spared him, or had it been something else that had saved him from death?

The pain poor Phae must have gone through as the dark mage's prisoner didn't bear thinking about. The very thought made him shudder.

Just what was he going to do?

He considered his two companions sleeping beside him. He hadn't just failed Phae: he had failed them all. He had become so consumed in his desire to rescue Phae, he had neglected the suffering of his two closest friends.

Slowly, silently, he raised himself to his feet. He needed some time to think...

* * *

The precipice was a cold and lonely place; far colder now the sun had faded and hope had left him. He stood for hours on the edge, looking out over the dark and foreboding sea that stretched out into the mysterious beyond. Somewhere in the ocean's depths his beloved Phae rested, never again to see the light of day.

Time seemed to stand still as he stood alone, silent and unmoving, the world passing by around him. As the hours passed his thoughts turned to Kiera. She had been travelling for many months now, and in all that time he hadn't heard from her once. This in itself was not unlike her – he knew how difficult it could be to send a covert message from one side of the Kingdom to the other. He knew also how important her task was – how crucial a part she played in keeping the realm safe from harm. Though she was doubtless many hundreds of miles away he didn't doubt for one second that she would feel the pain of Phae's passing. He had failed Kiera as much as he had failed Phae and he had failed his friends. He just wished he could see her; wished he could hold her. She'd know what to do. She always did.

He sighed as he wiped away a tear from the corner of his eye. Just then a figure approached him from behind. A hand rested on his shoulder. Callum turned to see Lena's reassuring gaze.

"I think it's time to go."

"Go? Go where?" For a moment, all thought left him.

"Asturia Callum; back to the Magical Isle. We need answers."

Callum paused. He had almost forgotten about Varrus and the fate of the 'Isle he had left behind. Compared to the fate of the wizards, his troubles were as nothing.

"Is Aaron up?"

Lena gave him a smile. "We've been up for hours Callum. We just thought you needed some time."

Callum nodded. He took a deep breath as he cast his gaze for a final time over that tragic scene. If they didn't find answers soon it would be far more than Phae that was lost to them.

He exhaled slowly. There was a long road ahead of them. There would be plenty of time to think on the way.

3

In his small office at the heart of the Wizards' Citadel, Elidor paced. Ever since Callum had left to rescue his daughter events on the 'Isle had gone from bad to worse. It had started not long after Callum first went away, when the residents of the 'Isle – himself included – had noticed a distinct change in the world of magic. Casting had become difficult, and required an extraordinary amount of extra focus just to produce the simplest of spells. Many of the less experienced magic users had lost the ability to cast completely.

That was when the panic began.

It started slowly at first, with just a few of the more senior mages coming to him and asking for his advice. They came one, or perhaps two at a time to his office, knocking politely and waiting for the previous occupants to finish their discussion before being ushered in by an aid to have him do his "uncertainty" speech all over again.

It had been fine at first, but as rumour spread of the death of magic, or in some cases, *the end of the world itself*, things soon started to deteriorate.

Weeks later and the residents of Asturia suffered the second setback in as many months. Even the most experienced magic users now struggled to cast. As if this weren't bad enough the fading magic also meant that many of the 'Isle's amenities started to fail. Magically-attuned street lamps for example, failed to light in the evening, leaving the city streets shrouded in darkness. People, quite naturally, grew scared, and it was all Elidor could do to try and calm them.

And then came the final straw.

Two days had passed since the third and final catastrophe, and if there had been even the faintest trace of magic left in the realm, it was now no more. The residents of the Magical Isle were left, just as their cousins on the mainland; devoid of magic and painfully aware of their own weak grasp on the thread of life. Without magic they were mortal, just like everyone else.

To the Seer, whose magical foresight had always been more of a curse than a gift, the future was now nothing but an endless gloom – an impenetrable black of uncertainty. His powers were no more, and this could mean only one thing...

Elidor stopped pacing in front of a large book cabinet and stared at his reflection in the glass. He took a deep breath and considered his options. Though his foresight was gone, he was most certainly not bereft of his wits. The death of magic had been the last part of his visions before they had faded completely. Given the current state of affairs it seemed certain that Callum and his companions had failed in their quest and had been bested by whatever dark force was at work upon the world. If they were still alive they would most likely try to return to the 'Isle. If they still lived there might yet be hope.

If...

Elidor turned away from his reflection and considered his next course of action. His own fate may well be sealed, but he certainly wasn't going to go out without a fight.

He walked over to the door and turned the key in the lock. A large crowd of mages turned and looked at him expectantly.

There was only one thing for it: he would have to send for help.

* * *

The bar was packed. Every which way Edwin looked his fellow recruits were drinking and making merry. Those who weren't sitting on stools or tables – or in some cases the bar itself – were standing tightly packed around where some clever soul had decided to pull some tables together and start the drinking trials.

He'd been fortunate enough to avoid the initiation thus far, but with the number of recruits who hadn't "run the gauntlet" rapidly wearing thin, he knew his turn was close.

Edwin edged his way closer to the table. In the crowded tavern his height made it difficult to see. Fortunately, his slight frame also made it easier to slip nearer the front. The challenge was just about to begin.

At the sound of a bell the latest plucky contender took his seat. The ringleader bellowed to the baying, drunken crowd. "Ladies and gentlemen, are you ready?" A raucous cheer rose around the tavern as the ringleader laid out cards on the table. He laid them in a diamond shape, one tip of the diamond pointing to himself, and one tip pointing towards the plucky contestant. Edwin craned his neck to see who the unfortunate soul was.

"Lukas?!"

Lukas looked up as he heard Edwin's voice but couldn't make him out amidst the crowd. Finally, Edwin forced his way to the front.

"Lukas you were supposed to be getting us a drink!"

"Sorry Edwin I got… distracted."

When Edwin saw the rather comely tavern girl at his friend's side he could tell why. Lukas always was one for bravado – and it was his bravado that often got him into trouble. Edwin gulped as he saw the row of shot glasses lined up along the table. His friend may have been the tallest trooper in the tavern, but for all his size Edwin knew from bitter experience he certainly couldn't handle his drink.

"Lukas you're going to make a fool of yourself."

Lukas stole a glance up at the tavern girl standing by his side. "Don't worry I know what I'm doing."

"That's what worries me," Edwin replied, as with these words the game began.

The crowd fell to a hush as Lukas turned over the first card. It was a six: he was safe.

One down, four to go.

He now had a choice of two cards to pick from. If he chose a picture card he'd have to take a shot and go back to the start. He picked the card on the right. A seven – brilliant! Three more to go. Edwin couldn't bear to watch.

Just then someone beside him spotted he didn't have a drink and forced a fresh pint of something into his hand. He received the frothy glass with a nod of thanks and took a sip. His head started to spin. He had drunk way too much already; he was treading on dangerous ground.

All around him, the recruits started to jeer: Lukas had picked another two non-picture cards. He now only had one card left.

Edwin closed his eyes. So far no one had completed the gauntlet without having to take a drink. The chances of doing so were exceedingly slim.

"Seven!"

Lukas looked up at the tavern girl and shot her a grin. She blushed as all around them, the expectant crowd cheered.

"Alright, alright, I'll do it again!" he declared. Everyone in the tavern cheered again. Everyone that was, except Edwin. By now his head was really starting to spin. He pushed his way through the crowd to try and get some air. Spotting a free stool in the corner of the bar he made a stumbling line towards it and slumped himself down at the table.

A slim blond-haired woman studied him curiously.

"Hello *hic*, thish shtool's not taken ish it *hic*?"

The woman shook her head and smiled kindly. "Not it isn't my friend – feel free to join me. It looks like you could do with a sit down."

Edwin steadied himself on the table and peered at the strange woman intently. There was something about her that wasn't quite right. "Hang on a second *hic*. You're not a recruit are you *hic*? Call it inshtinct *hic* but I can tell you know."

The stranger smiled. "Well it seems you've got me worked out. I'm certainly not a recruit that's for sure. Just came in from the cold to see what all the fuss was about. Old barracks tradition, is it?"

Edwin nodded and then wished he hadn't. The world started to spin and just wouldn't stop. "Yesh *hic*. Happensh every year *hic*. Initiation *hic* for the new recruits *hic* into *hic* the Kinsh army *hic*."

The stranger smiled. She was about to say something when Edwin beat her to it.

"Excuse me," he said with a start. "I think I'm going to be shick..."

* * *

Kiera watched as the young trooper stumbled his way to the door. She had been watching him for a while now and had already marked the group of sniggering fools who had spiked his drink. He was going to have a mighty headache come the morn that was for sure. She didn't envy *anyone* the task of reporting to the barracks the next day with a hangover like *that*. That was when the real initiation began.

Kiera rubbed her hands together to try and get some warmth into her fingers. It sure was getting colder outside – and to think it was Midsummer's day! Something was wrong, she knew that much. And it wasn't just the weather that was giving her cause for concern. For weeks now, she had been feeling "hollow" – empty almost – though at first she just put it down to home-sickness. It sure had been a long time since she had last been home, since she had last seen Callum and Phae.

She was just about to rise and check on the sick trooper when some commotion from the central table set her senses on edge.

She stood up and pushed her way through the crowd. She checked her sword was loose in its scabbard at her side. She wasn't going to draw it, but if she had to, it was good to know it was ready just in case.

Just then the crowd around the centre started jeering. One angry voice in particular raised itself above the tumult.

"Leave the woman alone!"

Experience told her it would only be a matter of moments before the first punch was thrown. If she didn't act now the whole tavern could erupt in violence.

Fortunately, the barman beat her to it.

"Oi, let go of me *hic*. That's my gal he's messing with!"

Kiera pushed her way to the front of the crowd just in time to see the tavern's two hired heavies seize a tall young recruit by the arms and start dragging him to the door. The trooper was massive – one of the tallest men Kiera had ever seen – and he was putting up quite a struggle.

The trooper's protests fell on deaf ears. "I ain't done nothing! *hic* It was him! *hic* Let go of me will you!"

As the trooper was dragged away Kiera noticed a sly looking character sneer in the young soldier's direction. He had his arm wrapped firmly round the girl from the bar.

Kiera sighed and turned towards the door. "When will they learn..." she muttered.

As she pushed her way back through the crowd one of the recruits tried to grab her by the arm. Kiera shot him a look so dark he immediately backed down. "Soldiers," she tutted.

Just then she reached the tavern door and moved aside to let the two heavies past. As she did she spotted the tall young trooper lying outside face down in the snow.

Kiera started.

The snow...

4

Callum woke with a jolt. Someone was tapping him on the arm. He groaned as he turned to see Lena sitting beside him, looking at him, a concerned look etched upon her face.

"You're doing it again," she said softly. "You told me to wake you the next time you did."

Callum looked down at his hands. Sparks arced between his fingers. He didn't even need to click his fingers anymore – it was almost as if the sparks had a will of their own. He frowned. If only he could work out what was causing them…

Just then the cart hit a bump in the road and the two companions were jolted in their seat. From the back of the cart a familiar voice let out a loud curse.

"Callum what did I tell you about your driving?!"

"Are you alright back there mister sleepy head?"

Aaron felt his way cautiously towards the front. "I'll have you know Callum I thoroughly deserved the nap I was taking, and certainly didn't deserve to be woken so rudely by yourself!"

"Well it wasn't me this time," Callum retorted. "And to be honest," he added sheepishly, "I was dozing too!"

Aaron cast his gaze accusingly in Lena's general direction. The water-mage held her eyes fixed on the road ahead.

"Before you say anything I know what you're thinking Aaron and it wasn't my fault. I got distracted that was all."

"Distracted by *what* exactly?"

"By this," Callum held his hand up to Aaron's eyes, but then quickly corrected himself. "By my fingers."

"You're not going on about that again are you?"

Callum nodded. "I'm not even clicking them now – they're sparking of their own accord."

"So if the magic's not coming from the world around us then there's only one place it can be coming from." Aaron replied. "You know where that is now don't you Callum."

Callum frowned. "What, you mean inside me?"

Aaron shrugged. "Where else?"

"But that's stupid – that's impossible – that's…"

"*Happening*?" Aaron suggested. Callum frowned once more.

Just then, Lena stopped the cart and turned in her seat. "Aaron you're a genius! Callum, don't you see – I think he's got it. It's coming from *inside you*. Do you know what that means?! It means, it means…"

Callum looked incredulous. "No, I can't be – that's preposterous!"

Lena and Aaron both looked at him in silence.

"No… Surely not…"

They continued to stare at him.

Callum looked down at his hands. As he moved to rub them together for warmth a large spark snapped between his palms.

He sighed as he let Lena pass him the reins while she jumped into the back beside Aaron. Whatever the reason, they had a long way to go before they found any answers. He just wished Kiera were with them…

* * *

Amidst the cold shimmering waters of the western sea, Asturia, the Magical Isle – the home of the wizards – was a forlorn sight as compared to the splendour of days gone by. As the unending twilight fell upon the realm, so the famous lights of Asturia began to fade. Like its people, the city had become but a shadow of its former self – a withered husk, drained of its power and sapped of its will to be.

On the furthest extent of the western wall, the city's guardian, the grey Seer, stared blankly into the dull mists out to the west.

On a good day he knew he'd be able to see the small rocky outcrop that marked a part of the island long broken apart. With the loss of magic the small lighthouse that stood sentry atop the "wizard's finger" no longer shone out as a beacon of the 'Isle's approach. With every night that passed

Elidor dreaded the sight of a wayward ship caught off course washed up against the rocks.

But that was the least of his worries. He breathed deeply and stared once more into the distance. Though he was without the power of his magical foresight, his long years of experience told him the final act was soon to come. He had been waiting all his life for this, his final moment; the time when the fate of the world would be decided once and for all.

Just then a messenger approached him from across the wall. The young apprentice bowed as he approached.

"There's someone to see you sir."

"Someone got my message?"

"No sir, she came of her own accord – said you could use the help."

Elidor nodded and followed the messenger along the wall to the steps that led down into the city. It would take over a quarter of an hour for them to reach the Citadel. Truth be told he was keen for the walk. Anything at all to generate some warmth in his old, tired bones.

He arrived at the Citadel to find the interior almost as cold as it was outside. Without the luxury of magically-imbued heating elements the wizards staffing the building had built up small fires in many of the main communal areas of the complex, but his own chamber was clearly not one of them.

He was pleased then to find a steaming cup of tea waiting for him on his desk. He was almost about to ask the young messenger to show their guest in, but then spotted her sitting comfortably behind his desk.

Elidor didn't need foresight to know the face hidden under the cowl. He could recognise Freya anywhere.

The Lintari stood as he entered, and vacated his seat. As she did, she allowed her hood to fall away to reveal a face that set the Seer's heart racing even now, over two decades since they had last met. She hadn't aged a day.

She was stunning – there could be no doubt. Yet despite her beauty, and despite her almost unrivalled talents, even for a member of the Lintari, her blue eyes held a deep sadness, a dark burden she had carried with her throughout her days.

"I hope you don't mind but I took the liberty of pouring you a cup of tea," she said as Elidor picked up the cup gratefully and allowed its warmth to seep into his fingers. He nodded his thanks.

"I drank mine while I waited."

There was an awkward silence for a moment as Elidor sipped at his tea and the Lintari seemed to struggle to find words. Eventually, she did.

"A darkness stirs in the west."

Elidor nodded glumly and placed his cup on the desk. "Your people can sense it too?"

Freya gave a dry, ironic laugh and gestured to the heavens. "Well my friend even if we couldn't I'd say the weather would suggest something was amiss."

Elidor conceded the point. "So you came here."

She nodded. "So I came here in search of answers and found the new master of the 'Isle away from home."

The Seer took another sip of tea and told her all he knew of Phae's disappearance. Freya's face was grim.

"This surely isn't a coincidence?"

Elidor sighed. "When you've been a Seer as long as I have my dear you stop believing in coincidences."

"And Aaron and Lena have gone too?"

The Seer nodded.

"And what of my sister?"

"I don't know," the Seer shrugged. "I certainly haven't heard from her. I can only hope and pray she is with them. The four of them together are far more powerful than they realise."

"Indeed."

As the Lintari considered all he had told her, Elidor took another sip of his tea. Though Freya's arrival on the 'Isle was in itself an ominous sign of the darkness to come, he found her presence reassuring nonetheless. Maybe *she* could advise him on the best course of action to take.

"It was good of you to come Freya."

The Lintari nodded, and offered him a faint smile. Before the Seer could speak again, a messenger burst into the office. She was breathing hard and her eyes were wide with fear.

"Sir, sir, come quickly – there's something in the sky!"

The Seer shot a glance at Freya and then back at the messenger. He slammed his cup down on the table and rose to his feet. Freya beat him to the door.

"Show me. Now."

The messenger nodded and hurried on ahead of them. She led them through a series of corridors and up half a dozen flights of stairs towards the roof.

They arrived to find a small group of mages gazing up to the heavens. One of the group held a looking glass to his eye. Elidor snatched it off him as he arrived and peered up into the sky.

High above them just below the layer of cloud, a large eagle-like creature circled.

Elidor adjusted the looking glass and brought the creature into sharper focus.

He soon wished he hadn't.

It wasn't an eagle at all – far from it. More reptile than bird the creature was at least twice the size of a man, and with its thick leathery wings extended, was perhaps twice as wide as it was long. A creature of the pit given mortal form, rows of jagged teeth lined its vicious snapping beak that gnashed and gnawed through the air as if biting at some unseen foe. What at first glance Elidor thought may have been feathers he soon realised were in fact thick, dark scales.

He handed the looking glass to his companion who studied the creature with interest.

"It's a scout," she said finally, "there can be no doubt."

The mage from whom they had taken the looking glass summoned the courage to speak. He trembled as he spoke. "Scout party for *what*?"

Freya looked at the Seer and raised an eyebrow. Clearly even now the possibility of the 'Isle coming under attack was just beyond some of its residents. It was an issue that sorely needed to be addressed. As if reading her mind the Seer responded with an expression that told her he knew the great task that stood before him. Deciding to let the point go for now at least, she continued on another track, "The question my friend is perhaps not so much what, but *who*."

It was now Elidor's turn to look startled.

"I take it you didn't spot the robed figure hugging closely to the creature's neck?"

The Seer shook his head, though from his expression Freya could tell perhaps he knew more than he was letting on. She looked at the three scared mages beside her and considered her words carefully.

"I think friend Seer, it's time you and I had a little chat…"

5

Edwin exhaled deeply, his breath billowing in the biting cold.

He put his axe down for a moment and risked a glance around him.

Three days. Three whole days they'd been chopping firewood to feed the great fires that had been set up in the squares and assembly points in Lambros. Three whole days and still the sergeant hadn't explained why half of them were chopping firewood, while the other half had been set to law and order duties in the city. At least that was *proper* soldiering.

Edwin sighed as he picked up his axe from the floor, dusted it of snow, and turned his attention back to the task at hand. All around him recruits strained and swore as even in its last gasps of life the giant leafy oak did its best to hamper its attackers.

Leafy.

It seemed strange to be turning an axe on a tree so abundantly full of life, still in its summer bloom; seemed strange to see snow covering fresh green leaves.

Beside him a particularly vigorous soldier cursed loudly as he caught a splinter in the palm of his hand. Edwin shot the trooper a look of sympathy. They'd all caught splinters somewhere or other over the past few days, but the trooper beside him seemed better than most at attracting injury, be it splinters in the hands or chunks of wood flying through the air and hitting him on the head. Somehow the young recruit just seemed to attract trouble.

It was just then that Edwin realised he didn't even know the soldier's name.

He was just about to introduce himself when a voice hailed him from across the clearing.

Edwin raised his head to see who it was, and grinned as he saw Lukas bounding towards him. Along with the biggest and strongest recruits, Lukas was part of the group charged with moving the felled trees on wooden runners to the chopping teams. Unlike Edwin, he didn't seem to feel the cold one little bit.

Lukas returned Edwin's grin as he stopped beside him.

"Have you heard the news?"

"What news?"

"Sergeant says we've just received rotation orders. We're to set down our things at once and prepare to move into the city."

Edwin carefully set down his axe and looked up at his towering friend. "Rotation orders you say?" He rubbed his aching back. "I sure could do with some lighter work."

"Well I'm not sure about lighter work. Word is it's the recruits in the city who need the rotation…"

Edwin raised an eyebrow. He gestured to the tired and weary faces all around them. "What on earth could be worse than *this*?"

Lukas shrugged. In the distance they could just make out the first line of soldiers marching out of the northern gate towards them.

For some strange reason Edwin knew he'd come to regret those fateful words.

* * *

Kiera frowned as she watched the long procession of soldiers file out of the city. She stood a little way apart from the assembled mass of troopers hard at work chopping wood, just far enough away to remain unseen and yet still keep the city in sight. Something told her she needed to have a good view of the city gates. Something was coming. No one had been able to tell just how long the cold spell would last, but with no foreseeable end in sight, things were starting to get tense.

The people were hungry. Summer crops had been spoilt by the cold and the stores were all empty. Winter was still supposed to be many months off yet, and they weren't even approaching harvest season.

A cold, hungry population was a dangerous thing. Kiera knew all too well how dangerous – how *volatile* – a starved population could be if pushed, and right now the young recruits were suffering because of it. It was certainly a harsh indoctrination into the life of a soldier in peace-time that was for sure.

She thought about the two young men she had met that cold mid-summer's day in the city. That had been the first day of the snow. There had been many more days of it since, and now in places the snow stood more than six inches thick. Six inches of snow in the middle of summer!

These were troubling times…

But wait! There, in the distance: a lone rider galloping towards the city gates. The horse seemed distressed. The rider was slumped forward over his mount and barely managed to keep control. He looked badly injured.

She offered a small prayer of thanks to the spirit of the earth for guiding her to this place so that she was among the first to see the rider coming into the city. Something told her that whatever news he brought, it wouldn't be good.

Without another moment's thought, Kiera started to pad her way softly towards the city.

By the time she arrived at the city gates, the messenger had already arrived and was in loud and somewhat disturbing conversation with the two guards. As the sound of the exchange reached her, Kiera could already see a small group of city-folk gathering at the other side of the gate. She moved a little closer to get a better view. The guards stumbled backwards as the messenger fell from his horse into their arms.

"Demons!" the injured man gasped, "They came from the sky… Giant leather-winged beasts with claws as long as your finger… Furies! They descended upon us from the heavens. They swarmed us from above. They took Ailish first – plucked her from her mount and bore her up into the sky. Her horse bolted as she was ripped away, but before I could see what became of her the demons set upon poor

Nathanial…" The messenger coughed. As the sergeant held the poor man steady his companion rushed to seek help.

"What happened? Where did they come from?"

"I… I don't know. Master Elidor warned us to travel with the greatest possible speed but I never for a moment imagined why. Maybe he foresaw it – maybe he knew they were coming *cough*. He sent us to warn you – to warn you all! 'The Dark Envoy cometh,' he said, 'and his armies will descend upon the 'Isle as the mighty Nu'il, the greatest of all rivers, sweeps down from the Kingdom's heart.' Unless we get help soon Asturia will fall and the Dark Envoy's armies will turn their attention upon the mainland."

The guard sergeant stood silent and incredulous as with a cough the messenger slipped into unconsciousness. Behind him the crowd of onlookers had swollen in number to well over fifty, and more and more were adding to their number as every moment passed.

Kiera watched as the sergeant placed the poor man on the ground and covered him with his coat. Unless healers got to the man soon the messenger may well have spoken his last.

Kiera breathed deeply as she considered all she had seen and heard – all she had felt – the past few weeks as the magic in the world had slowly ebbed and the light of the sky receded to dusk.

Her path was clear to her at last. She would accompany whatever support the King sent to Asturia. There she would find her husband and figure out whatever was going on. If the 'Isle was in danger then so too was her family and the realm's only chance of survival.

The fate of the world once more rested on the wizards and on one man she loved more than life itself.

"Callum…"

6

The trawler rocked gently as cold winds buffeted it from the east. Though a passenger craft by trade, its rooms were instead filled with provisions – crates of aid sent from the mainland to provide what meagre support they could for the residents of the ancient 'Isle. Aside from the small crew, the forlorn trawler carried only three passengers: two of whom stood out on deck, huddled together for warmth, lost in their own bleak thoughts.

Though he was without sight, Aaron stared out into the distance, out into the impenetrable dark that marked the boundaries of his world.

"A storm is coming."

Beside him, Lena stirred. "What makes you say that?"

"You can't feel it?"

"I can't feel a thing," she replied. Aaron nodded and squeezed her hand a little tighter. It had been a stupid question. They had both been struggling of late, but these last few days Lena had been suffering particularly. She had always been so strong, but now, confronted by the absence of her gift – the absence of her being – she was quite literally a shadow of her former self.

He let out a deep sigh. Lena stepped closer to him and allowed him to wrap his arm around her. Even her body felt cold.

Lena shivered.

"Are you sure you don't want to go inside?" Aaron suggested. "Callum's probably got the right idea you know."

Lena shook her head. "I want to see it. Not long to go now."

"Describe it to me. What can you see?"

Lena paused as she considered the grey storm clouds looming large in the distance. They were surpassed only by the even greater black blotch in the sky that cast the horizon – cast the whole *world* – in a perpetual gloom that filled her heart with fear. She considered telling Aaron a lie, telling him that everything was alright, that the 'Isle was safe and that the world would be saved.

As she weighed up her words, in the distance she could just spot the unmistakable shape of the Magical Isle growing in the distance. What was once considered one of the wonders of the ancient world was now no more than a lifeless shell, its life thread cut, its light shrouded by the eternal night. A tear formed in the corner of her eye. She was glad Aaron couldn't see *that*.

Aaron waited patiently for her response. She choked back a sob.

"It's… it's…" she buried her head in his chest. "It's awful."

Aaron breathed deeply as Lena finally succumbed to the welling emotions that she had held back for so long.

He placed a kiss on her forehead. He had no words of comfort for her now. How could he in such dark times?

Slowly but surely, the trawler continued on its way…

* * *

Elidor's face was grim.

He wasn't cut out for this. He had seen far too many winters in his long life, and this new winter was by far the worst. His bones were just too old. His knees creaked as began to pace. He shouldn't even have been there, standing alone atop the city wall. But he was looking for something, anything that might give him a sign as to what the growing storm might bring. Far down below him at the base of the wall a fire had been lit to warm the brave men and women who stood watch.

He could really do with joining them, but something told him he needed to be on the wall – needed to see what evil it was they were about to face.

He looked up as high above him the black storm cloud finally settled over the city and brought with it a darkness even more chilling than the eternal twilight they already endured. Though his foresight was no more, it did not take one of his gifts to tell that it was no ordinary cloud.

Along the wall members of the city watch gasped, and some even drew their swords as the darkness settled upon the city. If he had had one success over the course of the past few weeks it was expanding the city watch and bringing in aid from the mainland. Though resources were scarce, the pacts of years gone by still held strong, and even now ships full of soldiers from the coastal towns were arriving to bring added support to the Magical Isle's pitifully weak defences.

He just hoped they'd be enough.

No one had ever planned for a time Asturia might be without magic. Why should they? Magic was as great a certainty as life itself. It was the underlying constant in the lives of the people whose very existence depended on it.

A soldier approached him and offered him a cloak. Elidor took it gratefully and wrapped it round his shoulders.

"Shouldn't you be at the Citadel sir?" the soldier asked. "We'll be sure to send you word as soon as anything happens."

Elidor shook his head, never for a moment taking his eye off the swirling seas. He had to be there. He had to see.

He didn't have long to wait.

They came from the skies.

Winged demons the colour of the night, shrouded under the cover of the ominous cloud, swept down on leathery bat-like wings, striking at the defenders looking out to sea.

Somewhere along the wall, the first soldier died. A high-pitched scream pierced the night as two of the foul creatures, each about the size of a small child, seized a helpless soldier and carried him out to the sea.

Elidor gasped. It was far worse than he could have imagined. This was no ordinary threat – this was an evil drawing on a magic the likes of which he had never encountered. Demons weren't supposed to exist – yet here they were, hundreds of them swarming down from the sky.

Magic...

The thought played on his mind and nearly brought about his premature end as a group of clawing demons swooped down upon them. One young recruit, barely out of her teens, bundled him to the floor.

"Master Elidor watch out!"

Elidor's heart raced. One of the bat demons let out a wailing shriek as it was cut down and torn apart by a group of furious defenders.

Well at least they die like any other mortal beast...

Elidor struggled to his feet and drew his sword. Though he was old beyond counting, he was not yet without fight. As the defenders reorganised small groups banded together for mutual support. Even as they did so Elidor watched as another poor soul was ripped apart by the demons' vicious claws. He then watched wide-eyed as a young man no more than a dozen paces from him fell to his knees and died.

Somewhere in the distance, a bell began to toll.

Elidor searched round, desperate for some sign of leadership – some figure of authority ready to organise the panicked troops. He then realised they were all looking to *him*.

He felt woefully unprepared.

"Where are our archers?" he bellowed. "Shoot these abominations from the sky!"

Someone must have heard his order as somewhere amidst the gloom a single arrow flew up from the wall and hit one of the demons square in the chest.

Time seemed to stand still as the creature hovered in the air, seemingly unharmed, before it let out a gurgling cry and fell plummeting to the ground. A cheer rose up from the defenders on the wall. Those with bows sent more arrows up into the sky.

"Mark your targets!" Elidor shouted over the growing din of the battle. "Swordsmen defend the archers… and bring me some light!"

Someone, he didn't see who, handed him a burning torch. Just then another demon tried to swoop down at him, but as it did Elidor waved the flame in the beast's face. The fire startled the demon. It screamed as in the moment's pause two soldiers set upon it with their swords.

"More light to the walls – the foul creatures don't like it!"

Just then he felt strong arms grab him and pull him away from the wall. "Master Seer we've been looking for you everywhere," the Watch Captain said. "You're needed at the Citadel."

* * *

The Citadel was in chaos. Everywhere Elidor looked Sergeants and Captains were bellowing orders while orderlies scurried around fetching supplies and ferrying messages.

The far side of the main reception had already been turned into a sort of makeshift infirmary, and while the battle had only been raging for perhaps an hour, already the space was almost full.

He paused as he stepped inside the Citadel entranceway and took in his surroundings. Something was wrong, but he couldn't quite figure out what.

Then it struck him.

"Mages!" he exclaimed at once, striding towards the main reception. "There are no magic users here!"

As if to support his point, he was greeted at the main desk by a nervous looking officer already on the brink of nervous collapse. An hour in and already everything was falling apart around him.

The officer's face was awash with relief as the Seer approached.

"Ah sir, how very good to see you." The young man fought to control a stammer. "Things here are pretty chaotic."

Elidor nodded, not looking for pleasantries. "Report Lieutenant. Why do I see so many soldiers here when they are needed on the walls?"

The officer looked nervous.

"I… I don't know sir. The mages… said they were powerless. Some have fled to their homes; others have taken shelter in the Council chamber."

Elidor nodded, a burning rage in his eyes. He turned to spot a particularly aged looking mage crossing the concourse. He grabbed the old man by the arm. "Mages: where are they? Take me to them!"

The old man looked startled at first, but years of experience had gifted him with a great pragmatism.

"Immediately my Lord."

They entered the Council chamber to find a large group of mages gathered round the chamber's central platform. A nervous looking young mage stood at a lectern leading the group in some sort of prayer.

Elidor burst into the chamber and broke up the group at once. "What is the meaning of this?!" he bellowed. "This is not a time for *prayer* brothers and sisters – this is a time for action!" He cast his gaze around the room. "What pitiful, pitiful beings you all are. There are *men* – not mages – *men* giving their lives on the walls, and yet here you are doing nothing, allowing your city, your *home* to fall. What have you to say for yourselves? *What have you to say for yourselves*?!"

The chamber was silent.

Finally, one small voice spoke up. It was Zachias, an old and highly respected mage of the Order of the Eternal Frost. His voice was barely a whisper.

"But we are nothing oh Seer. Without our powers we are less than nothing. We pray here because prayer is all we have left."

"Fools! You are never without power; you are never without hope. Pray yes, but pray while you put your body to use and help save us from a fate far worse than death. To work with you, one and all. The city, nay the *world* needs you!"

With that, Elidor stormed out of the room. A few moments later, the first of the mages followed in his wake. It may not have been much, but at least it was a start.

7

Their journey by sea took longer than they hoped. Choppy seas and a darkness few Captains would have dared to come to port in meant the trawler crept its way into harbour with as little sail as the Captain could muster, and more than a small amount of luck. Lena stood as she had done for much of the journey, staring out into the distance, one hand gripped firmly to the hand rail, the other placed firmly in Aaron's own. Though she knew he was keen to learn what she saw, she did her best to delay her response. As she considered her words, Callum emerged onto deck to join them. His eyes were red and bloodshot. "Ready?" he asked.

Lena nodded.

They hurried down the boarding plank and along the pier towards an area where crates were being unloaded onto carts. Aaron looked anxious.

"What do you see? It's bad, isn't it? I can tell you know; you don't have to hide anything from me."

Lena stopped and sighed, pulling Aaron aside as carts laden with supplies ferried goods into the city – or what was left of the city at least, for the walls around the port were crumbled and blood-stained, and for all his lack of sight, she knew he wouldn't be able to avoid the awful smell.

As if reading her mind, Aaron spoke. "It stinks of death here," he said. "I smell battle, I smell blood, and most of all I smell death. Tell me, is it really as bad as I imagine?"

Lena shot Callum a glance. He too was at a loss for words. Just then she spotted a strange shape in the snow. She hurried over to it, dragging Aaron along with her. She soon wished she hadn't. A bat-like creature with thick leathery wings and row upon row of razor-sharp teeth lay in a frozen pool of its own blood. Lena started to retch.

"What is it? What do you see?"

Callum led his friend a few paces away from the creature as Lena recovered herself. Aaron waited patiently. "So Lena, what do you see? What's happened?"

Lena told him. She told him everything.

Aaron's expression remained neutral throughout. As she finished she looked anxiously into his blank eyes, waiting nervously for a reaction.

Aaron drew in a deep breath.

"Well, it's not as bad as I had *imagined*," he said at last. He wrapped his arm around her. Callum hailed a cart destined for the city and the three companions jumped on board.

Lena hugged Aaron closely. Whether his words were for her own benefit or not she didn't care. They would need his strength more than ever in the coming days. If the foul demon creature in the snow was anything to go by, things were far worse than she had feared.

As they entered the city proper, a familiar voice hailed them. Both Callum and Lena looked round, but before they could find the voice's source a hooded figure leapt up onto the cart beside them. Aaron didn't need to see her face to know who it was.

"Freya!" he exclaimed. The Lintari swordswoman allowed her cowl to fall back so they could all see her face. "It's been too long!"

"It's good to see you my friends," Freya said as she allowed Lena to hug her and Aaron, who was furthest from her, to clasp her by the hand. As he did so she noticed the distinct change in his bearing. Lena saw the Lintari's expression and did her best to explain.

"The loss of magic has affected us all in different ways…"

Freya's expression was sombre. "The Seer has told me all that has happened – all that he knows of the death of magic. What news do you bring?"

Callum, Aaron and Lena looked at each other and then back at the Lintari swordswoman. "It's a long story,"

Callum said at last. "I think this had better wait until we see Elidor."

Freya nodded.

"But tell us," Lena continued, "What happened here?"

"Well I fear that too is a long story my friends," Freya replied as their cart drew to a halt in the press of supplies queuing to get into the city. "However, as it seems we have some time on our hands I suppose I had better get started..."

* * *

Elidor slammed his cup down on his desk, splashing tea over a pile of important looking papers stacked neatly beside it. Lena reached down and picked up the first few sheets that fell to the floor.

"She's what?!" He stared wide eyed at Callum who just nodded sadly.

"She's gone," he replied.

"It's not possible, I don't believe it, I–" Elidor paused. "I'm so sorry Callum, this is truly awful I..."

Callum did his best to maintain his composure. He sucked in a deep breath. "Don't worry about it Elidor. Goodness knows I've done enough grieving of late. I – *we* –all need to be strong now the fate of the world rests on a knife-edge."

Elidor was lost for words. He stood up and started to pace. As he did so he knocked more papers from the desk. As she was already on the floor, Lena picked them up and placed them carefully back on the desk.

"I just don't know what to say. I never for a moment predicted a development such as this... To think Varrus would stoop to such a depth. To think he would have the *power* to do such a thing!"

"I can't help but think Varrus is the least of our worries," Lena interrupted "This whole thing is just too big for it to be the work of one mage – even one so powerful as Varrus.

Remember, while the rest of us have suffered as a result of his schemes, his powers seem unaffected."

Aaron placed his hand on her arm. "He isn't the only one to have been unaffected by the sources' closure," he said, looking towards Callum. Both Freya and the Seer turned in the direction of Aaron's gaze.

"Callum?"

It was now Callum's turn to be lost for words. With Lena's help he did his best to explain the strange sparks that flashed between his fingers. At Aaron's prompting, he also described how he had survived the fiery comets.

Elidor stroked his chin. "Interesting... interesting..." He turned to the Lintari. "Freya have your people ever heard of anything such as this?"

Freya shook her head. "Not to my knowledge at least friend Seer, though I am by no means a scholar of such things."

Elidor sighed and collapsed back onto his chair. As he did, Lena's beautifully stacked pile of papers fluttered back to the floor. She considered picking them up again but a look from Freya told her it probably wasn't a good idea. The Seer reached for his tea and drained the cup.

"This is all too much," he sighed. "Varrus alive, Phae dead, magic disappeared and an army of unimaginable evil beating at our walls. What on earth are we supposed to do?"

"Well we were sort of hoping *you* might be able to tell *us*," Aaron replied.

Lena rested her hand on his shoulder. Tensions were running high enough as it was, without adding further fan to the flames.

"What about the archives?" Callum suggested. "Surely there must be something here that can tell us how to restore the sources?"

Elidor sat bolt upright. "That's it!" he exclaimed. "I've been so preoccupied with trying to keep the city safe I almost forgot about the books we uncovered in the sanctum! If there's one final task left to me then I pray it might be discovering some way out of this mess. Come friends – to the archives!"

As he made for the door he turned and saw the papers on the floor. "Lena dearest, you couldn't do an old man a favour and pick those up for me, could you?"

Lena and Freya both shared a look as the water-mage leaned down once more and began to collect the spilt papers. It was going to be one of those days...

8

Varrus folded his arms and allowed himself a small sigh of satisfaction. Far below him, stretched out along the length of the coast, his vast army was arranged and ready for battle. To his left, along the island's northern shore, a horde of winged furies stood waiting his instruction, biting and gnashing their jaws in anticipation.

He had already unleashed an initial wave of the demon creatures, and if the results of the first attack were anything to go by, he might not even need to call upon the larger creatures he had added to the furies' ranks.

A little way down the shore his personal cadre of hell-forged demons loomed ominously above the smaller creatures. Of all his creations these were the most powerful, though it would be with his ceramic warriors that the war would be won.

Silent, relentless and incredibly strong, his ceramic constructs were all but impervious to traditional arms, forged as they were in the heat of the volcano. Though they lacked the speed and tenacity of the furies and other assorted demons he had conjured, the unbreakable constructs would serve him well in ripping the walls of Asturia stone from stone. He nodded his approval at the silent warriors that stood perfectly still and erect, awaiting his orders.

With a wave of his hand the formation closest to the water turned and started marching into the sea. As soon as the first wave was submerged the second turned and followed the first, slow step by slow step, implacably advancing into the deep.

Across the island the large winged beasts he had prepared especially for his final assault shrieked and hissed as the ceramic army started on its long march towards the Magical Isle. Though he could almost taste their ravenous hunger for flesh, they would have to wait a while longer, if his plans were to come together as he intended.

At that moment the familiar voice of the star-god boomed inside his head.

"You have done well my servant – you have achieved far more than I could have imagined for one such as yourself."

"It is my pleasure to do your bidding my Lord." Varrus trembled as he felt the star-god send a prod of pain into his body as if to remind him who was still in control. Varrus did not doubt for one moment the omnipotent being could easily snap him in two at the merest whim.

"Every moment that passes now I feel my bonds weaken and my prison bars fall away. The power you have wielded on my behalf continues to make me stronger. As my darkness spreads, so my power grows...

"The time is near Varrus – I can feel it. It will soon be time for my freedom."

Varrus bowed once more. Along the beach even the furies fell silent, as if touched in some way by the star-god's presence.

"What is my next task my Lord? What would you have me do?"

Skargyr paused. Varrus could feel a tremendous weight pressing on his mind. The hairs on the back of his neck started to rise. The forces of magic were building all around him.

As the power reached its crescendo, a vapour of magic started to form in front of him. After a few moments the magical cloud started to spin. Varrus took a step back as he was almost blown from his feet under the force of the whirling currents. Faster and faster the magic span until finally the magical bands started to form into a shape forged of the star-god's own dark will. As the vapour faded Varrus gasped as he beheld the shape of a black Pegasus – the rarest of all magical beasts, with black wings far bigger than the greatest of eagle's, and large ominous eyes that spoke only of death.

"Ride my servant, ride forth on this creature of death, and do unto others as they would have so done unto me. Destroy

the wizards Varrus. Destroy the realm of men and watch it burn as I prepare for my triumphant return. The souls of the fallen shall feed me Varrus. Nourish me and help free me from my infernal prison."

Varrus gulped and took a step towards the frothing creature that stood before him. *Death...* yes *Death* was a good name for this mount.

Varrus allowed himself a thin smile. "It shall be my pleasure my Lord Skargyr. It shall be my pleasure indeed."

PART 3

DARKNESS' END

1

Dawn – if it could even still be called that – had barely broken when the dark shape washed up on the shore. Pausing in her work, Petra placed her barely-filled bag on the ground and peered intently through the gloom to where the shape lay. Even from this distance her keen eyes could make out the outline of a naked body sprawled on the shore amidst the sea-weed and detritus the tide left in its wake.

She has seen it many times before. Every so often the bodies of the dead washed up on the long stretch of flat sandy shore of the bay. If the bodies hadn't already been dumped in the water naked, they were soon stripped of their possessions by the scavengers that patrolled the bay like vultures. For many, the small amount of money or the few possessions they managed to secure might even be enough to buy a meal.

To Petra and her poor family, to find a few coins washed up on the shore was like finding the greatest treasure on earth. Though she saw the body was naked, there was a chance it may have been washed up with other useful items she could take to use, or even sell in the market. She gathered her basket of cockles and hurried down the beach.

At the sight of the woman running, basket in hand, a group of beach prowlers who had been patrolling further along the shore also broke into a run. In the competitive world of the scavenger, timing was everything. If they beat her to the prize they could lay claim to whatever they found.

Petra shifted up her skirt and concentrated on not scattering her precious basket of cockles along the beach. If she lost them, whatever she might find washed up with the body would be all but worthless in comparison.

Suddenly, she stopped. As the naked body came into sharper focus she spotted movement. The body – the *woman* – was breathing. The shock almost caused her to spill her cockles, but sight of the other scavengers closing down on her soon set her into motion again, and even faster than before as she saw one of them flourishing a knife. In these desperate times she wouldn't put it past them to use the knife on the poor woman – or even on her come to that – if they thought the prize worth the price in blood.

Suddenly, all thought of collecting a valuable prize left her. Her mother's instinct compelled her to help.

With the poor naked woman in sight Petra ran as fast as her tired old legs could carry her. Two days without food made her unsteady, and she stumbled as she went but still she kept ahead of the scavengers approaching from the opposite end of the beach. She would not be beaten.

Just then the woman stirred. She turned her naked body onto her back and stared up into the grey sky. Her skin glistened as what little light the dawn offered reflected off the moisture on her skin. Though the soft curves of her figure were exposed to the biting cold she didn't so much as shiver. In fact, she seemed remarkably calm.

Petra approached the girl – for she now realised the young woman was not yet out of her teens – and offered her shawl.

"Are you alright miss? What happened to you?"

The girl turned and looked at her blankly. In an unnatural motion, she rose to her feet.

Petra took a step back. "Miss?"

The girl seemed to register some small part of what she had said. She shook her head and turned to face away from the obscured sun. Further down the beach the group of scavengers had stopped and were aghast at the naked beauty standing before them.

"I must go," the girl said softly, as with these words, a cushion of air lifted her from the ground and she floated into the distance.

* * *

The world passed her by as if she were in a dream. The feeling was not unlike that which she had endured for so long under the ministrations of the dark mage. A little way behind her

134

a small band of villagers and townsfolk struggled to keep up with her relentless pace. Every so often their members would change, as either they could no longer keep up, or as new members spotted her and joined the throng. Some of them even tried to speak to her but she couldn't tell what they were saying. Their lips moved but no sound seemed to come out.

Is this what death is like?

One desperate woman even held out a baby towards her. Either the woman was looking for a blessing, or she wished her child to be taken away. Maybe she was even giving it as a form of offering. Whichever the case, Phae could offer the woman no hope.

For reasons far beyond her understanding, she had been spared from death. She had fallen for what felt like an eternity until finally the freezing waters had taken her and dragged her under. As the last bubble of air left her straining lungs she had started to breath water, but for some reason she hadn't drowned.

The waters had taken her; they had embraced her and dragged her down to the sea-bed. At that point she had lost consciousness. Whatever the ocean had done to her, it had washed her up on the shore, and now the strange powers of the earth called her – drew her inexorably onward against her will.

She felt *different* somehow. Her body had changed during her time in the ocean. But it wasn't the physical change that worried her most: it was the feeling inside her head. It wasn't a voice as such, more an instinctive *feeling* – a sense of clarity and vision far beyond that which she had ever known before. Though she didn't understand the force working upon her, she could sense what it wanted. It wanted her to go somewhere. She didn't know where precisely, but she knew the direction. It tugged at her relentlessly, not giving her a moment's respite as it pulled her ever westwards.

For now at least, she just let the power take her where it wanted. It had, after all, spared her from death, and while she had some vague awareness of her own nakedness, the power warmed and protected her from the elements which so many of the townsfolk struggled to keep at bay.

As the day slowly passed by, her band of followers slowly dwindled and at last turned off the road and returned to their homes. Though night drew in, Phae was certain the strange force guiding her would not cease to pull her through the night.

She was bound now to whatever path the powers of the earth had set her on. It was going to be a long, long night…

2

The archives were strangely silent. Where normally Lena would have expected to see teams of mages working diligently at their desks, now all that remained were stacks and stacks of untended books. The more she thought about it, the more the thought of the empty archives made her sad.

She drew in a deep breath and turned her attention back to the task at hand. All around her lay scattered manuscripts and piles of notes she had furiously scribbled as she sought to make some sort of sense out of everything that had happened. Her current line of research followed a rather radical theory that the sources were not "sources" at all, but more like sluices, or dams that controlled the flow of magic into the world. From her perspective at least, the theory seemed sound, however many centuries had passed since then and the theory had fallen out of favour. Information on the subject was incredibly hard to come by; though at least she was having better luck than the Seer.

A short distance away, at a desk almost twice as large as her own, Elidor poured over countless maps and charts in an attempt to piece together the different pieces in the puzzle.

Realizing she wasn't going to make any further progress for the time being at least, she rose to her feet and wandered over to the Seer's desk. He looked up as she approached. "Has it ever occurred to you Lena that there's a remarkable amount of symmetry to the location of the three sources?" He pointed to a particularly large map of the realm, on which he had placed three red stones. Each stone, Lena knew, marked the location of a source. The Seer drew a line between each stone, forming a triangle on the map. "It's almost too perfect not to have some significance."

Lena looked at the map and looked at the stones the seer had placed. There certainly was something oddly symmetrical about the whole thing. At the triangle's centre was the Great Forest, often referred to as "the heart of the Kingdom".

Was there more to the forest than its name?

Lena took a long slow breath. In none of the texts she had read did it mention the Great Forest anywhere. She placed a fourth red stone at the triangle's centre.

Just then her thoughts were interrupted as a messenger entered the study area and passed Elidor a note. The Seer read it with interest.

"Callum says he and Aaron are about to take a tour of the wall if we are so inclined to join them."

"That sounds like a good idea," Lena nodded. "I could certainly do with some fresh air." She took a step away from the desk. "Are you coming Elidor?"

The Seer shook his head. "Oh no my dear, you better go ahead without me. Besides, I don't think my old bones can take much more of this cold weather."

With the Seer's words Lena made ready to follow the messenger on his way out of the archives. As she did, she turned just in time to see the Seer still standing in place, staring fixedly at the fourth red stone...

Lena left the Citadel to find Callum and Aaron standing outside waiting for her. Aaron handed her a thick cloak as she arrived.

"Thought you might be needing this," he said. "It's colder now than it's ever been." She took the cloak gratefully and hung it on her shoulders.

"Thank you. So, what's the plan?"

"Well Aaron here was getting restless, and while organising the city is all well and good we thought it was about time to take a walk along the wall. We assumed you would want to join us."

"We also guessed the Seer wouldn't want to come – hence why we only brought one extra cloak," Aaron added with a grin. "Didn't need foresight for that eh?"

Lena smiled. It was good to see Callum and Aaron in lighter spirits than they had been of late, though how much of it was a mask she couldn't quite tell. As they approached the western wall she spotted groups of soldiers huddled round small fires that were kept burning thanks to a constant supply of kindling brought up from the city centre.

"From Elidor's experience with the fliers we took his advice and concentrated our forces around sources of light and heat," Callum explained. "We also have teams of archers on standby for when the assault comes. Though the attack could come from any direction, both Elidor and Freya have been quite insistent the greatest threat will come from the west."

Lena nodded. She too had heard the Seer's reports, and trusted Freya's judgement on such matters more than anyone. Of all the magical folk touched by the crisis, the Lintari seemed least affected. She only wished she could say the same for herself.

"Where *is* Freya by the way?" she asked.

The two men looked at each other and shrugged.

"We don't exactly know," Callum replied. "Even after all these years she still prefers to keep to herself."

With these words they reached the base of the wall and climbed the stone steps to the top. Even their thick cloaks did little to protect them from the brisk sea air. Lena shivered. Aaron put his arm around her as she stopped to stare out into the storm.

"What can you see?"

"I… I see… *emptiness*; a great impenetrable darkness that spreads as wide as the horizon. You were right Aaron: I really can feel it now – a storm *is* coming. I just don't know if we have the strength to face it. I don't…" she began to sob. "I just don't know if we can win! Tell me Callum, tell me Aaron, tell me there's hope!"

Callum took a deep breath. The eyes of every soldier along the western wall were upon him. It was his turn to be strong for his friends.

"There *is* hope," he said firmly, "And it is to be found on these walls. While each and every one of us stands here and draws breath there is yet hope. We *will* stand together, and we *will* defeat whatever enemy the dark one sends our way." He paused as he let his words sink in. He had lost a great deal over the past few weeks but he'd be damned if he would lose hope now.

"There is always hope," he said firmly. Lena slowly nodded. "You just need to know where to look."

As if to support his words a sudden vision leapt to his mind – a ship.

He turned sharply and was nearly bowled over by a young messenger: "Sir, sir, a ship has been sighted in the east."

Lena gasped. Aaron squeezed her tightly. "Maybe there is hope after all…"

3

The trawler rocked violently. Edwin grabbed the nearest handrail to steady himself. It was all he could do to hold his sea-sickness in check as strong winds buffeted them from all sides. More than one trooper had fallen overboard already and he wasn't about to let himself do the same. Beside him, Lukas barely noticed the choppy seas as he stood staring out into the distance. He pointed to where a large ominous black cloud loomed over their destination.

"Look at that Edwin. Whatever do you think might have caused it?"

Edwin had little patience for questions he didn't have the answers to. He was more concerned with the task of keeping his rations down. As he regained his footing he looked in the direction his friend pointed. "Do I look like a mage to you Lukas? Do I look like a scholar? If I was I certainly wouldn't have joined the army that's for sure."

Lukas shrugged and ignored his friend's sarcasm. Most of it just washed over him anyway. "It looks kind of scary," the big man said.

Edwin sighed as he regretted his outburst. He took a deep breath as he contemplated the growing darkness in the west. "It does, doesn't it."

"What do you think we'll find there Edwin?"

"I honestly don't know."

"The sergeant says we're to expect the worst."

"Did he say what the 'worst' might be?"

Lukas shook his head. "He didn't say. He just said to be ready for it, whatever it may be."

Edwin gulped. The more he looked at the ominous black cloud the more he wished his sickness might return to distract him.

Lukas clasped him on the shoulder. "I'm glad you're with me Edwin. It's good to know there will at least be a friendly face with me when the time comes."

Edwin breathed deeply. Lukas was like the brother he'd never had. His parents had both died when he had been but a small child, so Lukas' family had taken him in and raised him as one of their own. Ever since those earliest days, they'd always watched out for each other, and now, with darkness looming on the horizon, they'd need each other more than ever.

He nodded as he patted his friend's hand. "We'll stick together, no matter what."

Though the trawler had been chartered strictly for military use, there was one other passenger on board that day. Across the deck, hidden beneath a thick hood, Kiera stood in silent contemplation. She watched the dark cloud approach with a strange kind of interest. The powers of the world were aroused and she could feel her blood stirring at the prospect of battle.

She turned now and considered the few hundred soldiers that filled the majority of the ship's deck. For most of them this would be their first taste of battle – and against an enemy even *she* wasn't prepared for. They were all too green – some in more ways than one – their only hope of survival resting in the hands of a grizzled Captain from the mainland. She watched as Captain Bridgemore paced the deck, speaking to soldiers, offering words of advice where he could. While some leaders might have been tempted to take a strict line with the recruits, Kiera could see the benefit of the Captain's approach. The young soldiers were scared enough already, without having the Captain add to their fear.

Somewhere in the distance, thunder started to rumble. Kiera turned her attention back towards the ominous black cloud. Just then, she flinched. There, from the depths of the storm, a swarm of dark shapes poured forth; hundreds of thousands of indistinguishable shapes riding the crest of the tempest to descend upon the helpless city below.

And their ship was heading right into the heart of the storm…

* * *

The boarding planks thumped against the dock. Edwin stumbled forward amidst the press of troopers surging towards the shore. Lukas grabbed him by the arm as he felt his feet begin to slip beneath him. He hadn't even stepped onto dry land and already he owed Lukas his life.

At the Captain's orders they edged their way along the packed pier towards the shelter of the city. It was then that the first shrieks pierced the air.

"Get down!"

Edwin leapt to the ground and covered his head with both his hands as six dark shapes flashed past them, shrieking and slashing. Edwin rolled onto his back just in time to see Captain Bridgemore locked in combat with the first of the monsters, sword flashing as the creature clawed and swiped.

As soldiers rushed to the Captain's aid the creature beat its leathery wings and drew itself high into the air. Edwin watched in horror as the beasts made another diving run.

Lukas held out his hand and Edwin allowed himself to be dragged to his feet.

"We need to get off the pier!" he yelled. His companion nodded. Edwin looked around him in confusion. "Where's the rest of our squad?"

In the panic of the furies' attack, they had been separated from their unit. Lukas pointed towards the edge of the city. "There, look."

Edwin drew his sword and followed his friend amidst the tide of troopers running towards the city wall. He risked a brief glance behind him and was heartened to see the Captain sticking valiantly beside the last soldiers to leave the ship.

"Edwin watch out!"

Edwin ducked as a creature swept past him, scraping its talons mere inches from his head. Lukas sliced at it with his sword as it passed. The foul beast hissed furiously as Lukas' blade drew blood. The creature circled round and made as if to swoop down again, but by now the soldiers had organised enough swords to make the beast wary. With a piercing shriek the screaming fury flew back towards a larger group of beasts massing in the distance.

Edwin panted hard. In the space of a few minutes he had seen horrors the like of which he could never have imagined even in his darkest of dreams. To make matters worse it wasn't even *men* they were fighting, but creatures from some cruel nightmare. "What... what are they?"

Lukas shook his head. "I don't rightly know," he replied. "Strangest creatures I've ever seen that's for sure."

Edwin was about to speak but something tore his attention away from the conversation. He was sure the woman from the tavern had just brushed past him...

* * *

Kiera suppressed a shiver as she hurried through the mass of soldiers that filled the quay. Thankfully the attack had been only a minor distraction, and the Captain had successfully organised his troops in such a way as to come away from the skirmish with minimum casualties. The next battle would not be so easy.

She pulled her hood low over her face and hurried into the city. She needed to find Callum.

4

The fighting on the western wall was intense. Soldiers banded together to try and stave off the furies' attacks as every so often one of the larger beasts would swoop down and send the defenders scattering in all directions. The Magical Isle hadn't seen such bloodshed in many long centuries, and still the dark mage was yet to make himself known.

Callum allowed himself the briefest glance up at the sky as all around him men and women fought and died against a foe he couldn't even begin to describe. The fate of the world was balanced on a knife-edge and the furies were just the first move. Though his sword was covered in the blood of at least a dozen victims, the creatures continued to swell in number and swarm the walls in greater and greater numbers.

Just then his thoughts were brought crashing back down to earth as beside him, Lena let out a scream. A large creature, quite unlike any demon Callum had seen landed in front of them and let out a blood curdling cry. Aaron swore as the monster unleashed a wave of energy that swept him from his feet. A moment later and Lena fell down beside him.

Callum bounded over and helped his friends to their feet. Without his magic he was all but helpless against the terrifying beast. Just the look of the thing made his blood run cold. In that single moment, he realised his life was about to come to an end.

Lena let out a faint sob. "No… not like this…"

The creature advanced.

Aaron faltered. "Lena my love, if we don't make it through this know that I love you with all my heart."

Callum didn't get a chance to hear Lena's reply as from nowhere a shadowy figure sprang from the melee and dashed at the creature's flank. The monster let out an unearthly cry as the shrouded figure struck again, this time at the creature's other flank, removing a limb and slashing a powerful strike across its chest.

However, the creature timed to respond the lithe swordswoman countered and struck back – first at one leg, and then at the other. As the creature finally succumbed and tottered in its last gasps of mortal life, Kiera swung her blade and removed the creature's head.

A cheer rose up along the wall. At that moment the defenders were given the faintest glimmer of hope.

Callum stepped forward as he finally set eyes on his wife for the first time in months. A wave of conflicting emotions hit him all at once. The moment their eyes met, she knew the truth. She turned pale.

"Callum, where is Phae?"

The tears were already streaming from his eyes. "Gone," he whispered.

Callum struggled to find some words of comfort or explanation but found none. Though he thought he had cried himself dry in the long dark nights of their journey, tears started to stream down his face.

Kiera was perfectly still. She was in shock. Callum's words seemed almost without meaning.

Gone...

For those few brief seconds the world seemed to stop. The battle fell silent. Callum looked down into Kiera's eyes. "I'm sorry," he whispered.

"So am I," she replied.

All of a sudden, time returned to normal. It took Callum a few heartbeats to remember where he was but he was just quick enough to raise his sword to defend the redoubled efforts of the furies swarming them from above.

He glanced across to Kiera but was horrified to see she hadn't moved.

"Kiera look out!"

Callum's words fell on deaf ears. The furies swarmed, sensing a weakness in their foe. Before she could recover her senses, Kiera was knocked to the floor. Three ravenous demons fell upon her, pinning her to the ground.

Lena screamed.

Though he couldn't see what had happened, Aaron cried out, "Kiera!"

Callum was paralysed with fear. His whole world was crumbling around him.

Over the din of the battle he could just make out his wife's final words. "Callum, I'm sorry…"

Thunder rumbled overhead. Lightning crackled across the storm-filled sky. All at once clarity filled Callum's mind. A surge of power rushed through his veins. He had been powerless before – but never again.

Suddenly, the ground started to shake. Lena stumbled and was caught in Aaron's arms. Everywhere about them the battle paused as magic surged through Callum's body. His eyes burned a deep crimson red. He pointed at the three demons atop his beloved wife. His voice was as cold as steel. "Be gone!"

A blaze of lightning struck out from his palm, throwing the creatures aside. Somewhere along the wall, a soldier cheered. As Callum shot another bolt of lightning into a group of furies a further cheer spread along the wall.

Kiera shakily pulled herself to her feet. It was a miracle she was still alive. She looked at Callum and looked at her two friends standing a few paces behind him. The look on Lena's face told her all she needed to know.

She had always had an inkling – an instinctive sense – of the power her husband possessed, but she had never truly appreciated it until now.

Somehow… somehow, he had drawn on magical power that by all rights should not exist. She watched with strange fascination as Callum turned his face towards the blackened sky. "Are you watching Varrus? Are you watching?!"

All along the wall the soldiers redoubled their efforts.

The master of the wizards had returned.

* * *

The fighting was bloody. They had only been on the island for a few hours and already they had seen enough death to last a lifetime. Edwin stepped gingerly past the bloodied corpse of their sergeant who lay face down alongside three more of their former squad-mates. The four men had been cut down within the space of a minute by a particularly bloodthirsty pack of the smaller creatures that had forced them away from the harbour, into the city streets. If it hadn't been for Lukas and a couple of the braver members of their squad, he too might have fallen to their savage claws. By all rights he shouldn't even have been alive, but somehow he had survived where other braver, stronger men had failed. He was just one of the lucky ones, though he wasn't sure if "luck" was the right word for it.

As the adrenaline of their latest encounter started to fade, one trooper started to vomit onto the side of the street. Edwin patted the young man on the back as he stepped past him to find Lukas staring up into the sky. For some reason the demons had ceased their attack on the harbour and were heading for the western side of the island. Lightning flared in the direction the creatures were heading.

"What are you thinking?"

Lukas frowned. "Something's happening in the west. That lightning's not natural."

Despite himself, Edwin couldn't help but find his friend's comment amusing. He let out a laugh. "Not natural you say? Lukas this whole thing is 'not natural'! There are hundreds upon thousands of nightmarish creatures pouring from the sky. In all honesty I'm struggling to find anything *natural* at all!"

Lukas sighed as he kept his sight fixed on the source of the flashes in the distance. They seemed to be getting brighter.

Just then a strange sound caught his attention. It sounded like a horn. He turned to Edwin.

"What was that?"

"I don't know – I think it came from the harbour."

As the two men paused a trio of swordsmen ran past them in the direction of the docks.

"What is it? What's going on?" Edwin shouted to the troopers.

"The beach! The beach! A new enemy at the beach!"

Edwin caught Lukas' eye. Instinctively both men broke into a run. As they did the horn sounded again. From the ruins of the side-streets a dozen more troopers emerged, all running in the direction of the beach that ran directly beside the docks.

"I don't like the sound of this one bit," Edwin muttered. Lukas nodded, conserving his breath as they overtook a team of mages carrying packs of arrows and rations to the front lines. "Whatever do you think it could be?"

Lukas shrugged. "Don't know. Sounds bad."

Silence followed as the two men reached the edge of the harbour where a group of swordsmen were already forming into a line ready to repel the new invaders.

It seemed they were too late. At the watchtower almost a dozen soldiers circled a lumbering automaton, shaped like a man but almost twice the size, and with skin as hard as stone. The giant beast swung its sword in wide arcs, forcing the defenders back as it strode slowly, inexorably towards the dock.

Edwin looked on wide-eyed as a pair of soldiers died to the construct's blade. Even Lukas faltered in his stride. "What... what is that thing?" Edwin asked.

"I don't know. Look there, more of them. Edwin, they're coming out of the sea!"

Edwin looked to where his friend pointed and counted at least a score of the lumbering constructs slowly rising from the deep to set foot on the pebbled, sandy shoreline. One by one the strange ceramic warriors – more like walking dead than demons – assembled on the shore and joined their brethren in a single implacable advance towards the harbour.

Suddenly Edwin's thoughts were brought sharply into focus as he spotted a trio of soldiers, one man and two women, fighting desperately against a single construct. A piercing scream filled the air as the male soldier died to the creature's blade.

"Quick Edwin, we've got to help them!"

The two men broke into a run, but already Edwin knew they would be too late. The two women, enraged by their companion's death, ducked and darted round the beast, screaming furious war cries as they struck at the construct's flank. The ceramic warrior barely even noticed their attacks. With one powerful swing of its fist the first woman was sent hurtling through the air. The second woman barely had a moment to react as the impervious ceramic warrior ran her through with its blade.

Lukas skidded to a halt. Edwin stopped beside him and swore loudly. "We can't stop them," he cursed. "What do we do?"

In the distance, the flashes of lightning drew closer. A t that moment the ceramic warrior spotted them.

Edwin turned to his companion. There was fear in his eyes.

"Lukas, what do we do?"

"I… don't know," the big man replied. For the first time in all their long years of friendship Edwin saw that Lukas was genuinely scared.

The ceramic warrior approached.

"Oi you two, get over here!" The voice of Captain Bridgemore snapped them out of their terror.

Edwin and Lukas both turned. A short distance away the Captain stood at the head of a dozen or more men, a hefty warhammer in each hand. Behind him Edwin could see wherever they could, the soldiers had swapped their blades for weighty, blunt instruments. "We may not be able to fight them with swords, but I'll be damned if I let that stop me!"

The Captain handed one of his warhammers to Lukas. "Sorry I haven't got much else," he said as he saw Edwin's expression. "This was all I could find at short notice. Thank the gods the local smithy was working on these old relics eh." Edwin gulped. Even Lukas looked doubtful.

Again, lightning flashed in the distance, silhouetting the Captain against the dark storm-filled sky. The Captain turned, and raised his hammer in the air.

"Come on then – do you want to live forever?"

Edwin was about to make a flippant reply, but then thought better of it. He could see the look in the Captain's eyes. If they were going to die, they might as well die fighting.

Lightning flashed again. Either the storm was picking up or there was some new evil about to face them. Edwin tried his best to block the thought from his mind. He locked his eyes firmly on the Captain's back as together they charged the nearest construct.

At the soldiers' approach the ceramic warrior turned. It raised a powerful arm ready to dash its attackers away. The Captain ducked the blow and the two men beside him jumped aside. A third man, a little larger and slower to react, was knocked to the ground but quickly got to his feet. As the automaton swung its sword arm the first hammer blow hit, and was followed by half a dozen more in quick succession. A normal man would have died ten times over under the flurry of attacks but the ceramic warrior barely seemed to notice. It swung its sword and nearly removed one soldier's arm as Edwin bundled the man to the ground.

The Captain bellowed loudly as the two men struggled to their feet.

"Be gone foul demon!"

Slowly but surely cracks started to appear on the construct's surface. "Keep it up men – the creature weakens!"

Edwin jammed his sword into a large crack that was forming on the construct's back. He could only push it in a little way at first, but as the crack widened his plunged his blade through into what he could only imagine was the foul creature's heart.

The ceramic warrior stopped moving. A rain of blows continued to fall upon it, but it was as if piercing the creature's skin had cut the thin thread of life that kept it in motion. The troopers let out a cheer. A couple of them clapped Edwin on the back. He didn't feel like much of a hero, but in that moment, he had helped defeat one of the toughest foes imaginable.

However, their celebrations were not to last long. As the first of their number died, a dozen pairs of dead, otherworldly eyes turned to face the small band of desperate soldiers.

Edwin swore. It seemed their day was going to get a whole lot worse.

In the distance, the lightning grew ever closer.

5

Callum floated on the crest of a wave. The power he had unleashed surged through his veins, illuminating the twilight sky in flashes of dazzling light followed by equally dazzling dark light – the stuff of the malevolent powers – the stuff from which Varrus' armies seemed to be built. He floated a few yards from the ground, a shining beacon of hope to the men and women who fought valiantly alongside him.

This, Callum realised, must have been part of Varrus' plan all along – strike at the heart of magic and stop any chance the old world might have of saving itself.

Below him, following as closely as they dared, Kiera, Lena and Aaron stuck in close formation and fought desperately to keep the hordes of winged furies at bay. Callum knew now that he was the key – that he had been the key all along. By destroying *him* and all those dearest to him, Varrus would effectively win the day.

But Varrus' plan would be his undoing. Phae was gone, and Kiera had nearly died. Such had been the effectiveness of Varrus' scheme that Callum had almost succumbed. And yet crucially, he *hadn't* – and in the process, had unlocked the secret buried deep within him.

With vengeance in his eyes he unleashed wave upon wave of fiery comets into the furies' midst, culling great swathes of the dark creatures from the night sky. Yet still more of the demons continued to appear from above.

But it wasn't the furies that concerned him. There was something more – something far deeper and far more foreboding than the teeming swarms of demons laying siege to their homeland.

He paused and stared into the distance, stretching his magically-enhanced sight as far as it would allow through the infernal twilight. Something stirred in the east. A new enemy emerged from the sea. If he didn't act soon, the war might yet be lost.

With a signal to his companions, he floated towards the harbour.

* * *

Edwin cursed loudly. His body ached and he was covered in the blood of friends and enemies alike. Out of nowhere the winged demons had returned and set upon them, forcing them back towards the city while the slow, lumbering constructs followed in their wake, cutting down any soldiers unfortunate enough to stand in their way.

Beside him, Lukas was as caked in blood and dirt as he. Since they had cut down the first of the undead constructs their small band of fighters had been reduced by a further three. They now numbered just eight in total, and barely had the strength to face off against another construct should they encounter one.

Edwin's mood was grim. "Well Lukas, I fear this may be it."

Lukas clapped him on the shoulder. "It was fun while it lasted brother."

At these words a score of furies surged down upon them and seized another of their band, raising the poor man up into the sky before tossing him helplessly to a hideous, screaming death. Between the furies, the constructs, and the larger creatures that harried them, they were being forced further and further away from the port and into the city streets. They stood now at the edge of the assembled defences. A hundred yards or so to their left a further band of grizzled defenders did their best to make a fighting retreat towards them.

Another flash filled the horizon; then another.

"When those flashes reach us, I'd say that's us done for," Edwin sighed. Not even the Captain was inclined to disagree.

"You've done yourselves proud troopers."

Lukas paused. "What do you think it's like sir: death I mean?"

"I don't know son, I–"

The flashes repeated – even more intense than before.

Edwin's entire vision was filled now with bright ethereal light. He shielded his eyes.

"Look Edwin, it's come for us, it's…"

Edwin squinted hard as from the centre of the light a figure floated towards them. Death was now only a moment away.

* * *

Lena watched in mute fascination as she witnessed the birth of a power unlike any the old world had ever known. Callum had long been the most powerful mage in the realm, but now he had become something so much more. He wasn't so much a source as an avatar of magic – a living embodiment of the earth's power, floating through the air, a hundred small pebbles orbiting round him like some strange god from another age.

As they approached the first of the ceramic constructs the stones circled faster and faster until with a flick of his wrist Callum sent them hurtling towards it. The construct shattered, crashing into a million tiny pieces before Callum drew the stones back and sent them to the next construct, and then the next. Even the furies stopped in their assault as the stones cut through beast flesh and ceramic armour alike.

As the last of the constructs died Lena joined her companions as they followed Callum towards the small band of bloodied soldiers who even now stood firm, awaiting their fate.

* * *

High above the misery and destruction, Varrus, the dark envoy, appeared amidst a cloud of thick black smoke. His mount *Death* snorted furiously as he held position above the Magical Isle and surveyed the carnage his forces had wrought.

"Curses! What has he done to my beautiful army!"

Even from a distance the dark mage could sense the tremendous power being wielded so very far below. Every so often a flash of pure brilliant light would shine up from the 'Isle and cause him to flinch away in pain. Despite the cold, despite the dark, despite *everything*, somehow Callum had managed to find a way to thwart his plans.

Varrus could feel the lurking presence of the star-god at the back of his mind. He was now entering a critical phase of the plan. Failure now wouldn't just mean death – it would mean an eternity of damnation at the whim of his omnipotent master.

Varrus gripped the reins of his dark Pegasus tightly and brought his mount lower over the island. At his presence, swarms of furies and other foul creatures of the underworld flocked towards him and circled closely as he considered his next move. He did have one final gambit to play. If it succeeded it might just buy enough time for his master's final escape.

Death snorted wildly as Varrus took the beast into a sharp dive. Lightning crackled from the Pegasus' horn, flashing and sparking as they sped through the air. If he timed his plan just right, his armies would be inside the city before any of the defenders had a chance to react.

If...

* * *

Out of the blackness a massive wave of demons fell upon the defenders. Freya watched helplessly as one trooper was thrown from the wall only to be set upon by a dozen or more of the creatures that ripped at his flesh and tore great chunks of meat from his battered corpse.

Soldiers from atop the wall threw spears down at the creatures but for those short few moments the furies had no thought for anything save the prize of fresh meat. It was almost as if the creatures held no fear of death. It was almost as if they were something *different* altogether...

Freya had no time to think on the subject she scanned the streets for her next target.

Ever since Callum and his companions had arrived in the city and focussed their efforts on the city walls, she had patrolled the streets, watching, waiting for the first raiders to slip past the main defences in search of easy prey. Her swords were already slick with blood, and they would be coated further still before the day was out.

She flinched as out of the corner of her vision a pack of furies stormed from the sky. Their howling shrieks sent a shiver down her spine. She turned to face the direction of their flight and instantly caught sight of the small band of mages defending a cart laden with supplies for the front line. As the furies flew at the mages they formed a loose circle around their cart and drew what weapons they had. Without magic they were all but helpless.

Freya broke into a run. She vaulted a narrow alleyway and maintained her stride as she flew like the wind towards the savage creatures. With one final burst of speed she was upon them, blades whirring as she grabbed the nearest beast and dragged it to the ground.

Despite the speed and ferocity of her attack, the creatures reacted quickly. The beating of wings alerted her to one beast flying at her from her side. Instinctively she brought her right-hand sword up to block the swiping claws before she even registered the attack in the forefront of her mind. She fought on instinct now; before she knew it three creatures lay dead at her feet. There was a terrible shriek as the remaining creatures bore down on her.

She turned to the bewildered mages. "Run!" They looked confused. If they were slow to react it was because her own body was working at such speed. In the back of her mind she noted that they were slowly coming to their senses. She didn't have time to watch them but she recognised that her message had got through. She could now face the remaining furies without any distractions.

The creatures dived.

Freya whirled her swords in wide arcs and deflected the slashing blows. As the first creature passed her she landed her left sword in its back, allowing its momentum to drag her through the air and swing her second sword at its partner. A gnashing head fell to the floor.

There were now only three beasts left. Suddenly the creatures started to falter. Though they weren't born of the mortal world, they remained pack beasts at heart. Freya could sense their fear before they began to make a break for the heavens. She cursed her missed opportunity, but gave thanks for the lives she had saved.

Through the dim twilight she could just make out the shape of the mages' cart disappearing into the distance. Her work was done.

With a few sharp strides she approached the nearest wall and vaulted up onto it. With almost unnatural agility she glided along the wall and sprung up onto a low rooftop which led up to higher buildings beyond. As a child she had been swift; as an assassin she had been agile; as a Lintari she was unsurpassed.

A few swift leaps later and she was back among the rooftops, tracking for her next target. Lightning flashed overhead. A dark shape flew through the air raining death and destruction upon the helpless defenders. She turned and faced the direction of the port. She could sense the presence of another.

The next few hours would determine the fate of the world.

6

Phae shivered. Strangely, it wasn't the cold that made her tremble; it was the chill of magic pulling at her soul. She had been travelling for over a week, floating as naked as the day she had been born, pulled by some strange force that whispered to her in her dreams – comforted her and told her everything would be alright.

Given all her experiences it seemed strange that she should trust the force now guiding her, but something about it just felt "right". Somewhere deep inside her soul, she recognised the voice that spoke to her. Some small seed, planted there by her mother's blood had given her a direct link to the strange power that had saved her.

No, the power wasn't strange – it was perfectly natural.

Phae shivered again as the pieces of the puzzle started to fit together. She had undoubtedly gained her magical talents from her father, and from her mother she had gained... *the link.*

The earth was calling her, and it was a voice too powerful to resist. She travelled, she knew, to the Heart – a place so steeped in magic even the dark one would struggle to blot out its light. There she would reignite magic in the old world and right the wrongs of the past.

Phae closed her eyes and let the power of the earth continue to pull her westwards. She would need every ounce of energy she could muster for the challenges ahead.

* * *

Thunder rumbled overhead as the heavens opened to unleash a storm unlike any seen before. As the tempest grew, the entire force of Varrus' armies descended upon the city, and the sky teemed with the gnashing creatures of the night.

A bolt of lightning struck the western watchtower and set it ablaze. A group of soldiers who had taken shelter in the tower ran for their lives as the fire drove them into the waiting clutches of the hellish furies.

Callum poured all his energy into trying to save the fleeing men and women – freezing and burning the furies in equal measure as he drew upon the new forces of nature at his disposal. But even with his best efforts a trio of brave souls were plucked from the ground and torn to shreds by the ravaging beasts.

Callum turned as he thought he heard someone calling his name. Below him Kiera fought like a woman possessed. Each swing of her sword cut down another beast, yet it was never enough. Beside him, Aaron and Lena were almost helpless against the onslaught. As the battle gained in intensity, Kiera pushed herself like she'd never pushed herself before to keep her friends alive. Between swings she pointed up into the heavens.

"He's here!"

Callum turned his attention to the sky. There, amidst the unholy swarms, Varrus rode on a steed of the underworld – a dark Pegasus, cruel and unimaginably powerful. Callum raised a hand to shield himself as lightning arced from the beast's horn and almost struck him.

From high above them, Varrus cackled wickedly. "Like that do you boy? You'll be joining your daughter soon enough…"

A wave of comets flew from Callum's outstretched hand, but the dark mage swatted them aside. Varrus then responded with an attack of his own, unleashing a ribbon of deep purple energy that ripped into the beleaguered line of defenders, cutting a group soldiers to shreds where they stood.

"Don't worry boy, it'll be your turn soon enough."

Suddenly a scream from below alerted Callum to a new danger. Emerging from the city streets behind them, a dozen or more withered looking demon trolls strode onto the battlefield, striking left and right, sending the defenders into disarray. Lena was thrown from her feet. She landed without a sound – her body limp and motionless. Callum's eyes widened, fire raging within him.

Aaron dashed as best he could to Lena's side. As he did, a group of furies separated him from Lena and the rest of the battle line.

"You can't save them all boy – who will you choose?"

Callum watched in horror as Kiera became swamped in the melee. Aaron meanwhile stood alone and helpless over Lena's slumped form. It was his wife or his best friend. Which one would it be?

Varrus cackled again as Callum dived to Aaron's side and scooped Lena up in his arms. With all the strength left in his body he propelled the three of them high into the air and down again a short distance from the immediate danger. In an instant he turned his attention back towards where he remembered Kiera had been standing, but for the briefest moment he lost her amidst the chaos.

"Kiera? Kiera?!"

As the smoke of the battle cleared he just spotted the unmistakeable figure of his wife alongside another – Freya.

Callum breathed a sigh of relief as sight of the Lintari swordswomen fighting together gave him a brief moment of hope. Beside him, Lena was slowly coming to her senses.

"What... what happened?"

"No time to explain," Callum replied. "We've got to get out of here. Varrus is too strong there's just too many–"

He caught sight of his wife cutting down one of the demon trolls. "Kiera we've got to fall back!" She nodded with gritted teeth as the furies resumed their assault. It was all just too much – even for her.

Callum rose into the air and looked desperately for inspiration. Just then his eye settled on a familiar figure running towards them through the streets.

"Callum, Callum – I've got it! I know how to stop him!"

"Elidor, what are you doing out here? It's not safe it's–"

In his haste Elidor stumbled.

All at once the world slowed down. Cut off from the main force the Seer was an easy target for the winged furies. Before Callum could do anything to stop them, Elidor was borne up into the air.

"You've got to restart the Heart – only you can do it." There was a pause. "Pray for me…"

With his final three words, Elidor, the grey Seer died. Callum's world began to spin. All sense of time and space seemed to leave him as he sank to the ground. A familiar hand reached out and touched his arm. Lena's voice was remarkably calm.

"The key is at the centre. I guessed it before, but maybe Elidor was right. If there's something there – something that can save the world – then you need to go there now and bring an end to this evil. Only you–"

Lena's words were cut off. Suddenly there was a pause in the fighting. High above them, the dark mage screamed in rage.

"No! It cannot be! She can't… she…"

The dark mage kicked his mount into motion, racing eastwards away from the battle. The furies around him flocked in disarray.

Callum looked at Lena and then at Aaron.

"Where's he gone?"

Just then, a pair of figures emerged from the gloom.

"There has been a shift in the world," Freya said. "We can feel it."

"A shift? But what? Where?" Aaron asked.

"Magic," Lena replied. "Something's changing. I can feel it now." She turned to face Callum. "You must go. Elidor was right – the centre holds the key. It's the beating heart of the Kingdom. It's…"

"Varrus!" Aaron exclaimed. "That's where he must have gone!"

Freya turned to face Callum. "You must act at once if there is to be any hope of victory." She looked to the heavens. "Tarry much longer and I fear the world shall fall."

Callum faltered. "But I can't go on my own. I–"

Kiera stepped forward. "I'll come with you," she said confidently. "I left you before; never again."

Freya nodded. "It is a wise choice."

Callum turned to face Aaron and Lena. They were battered, bruised and caked in blood and dirt. To think neither of them had slept in their own bed since that fateful morning when he'd come knocking on their door. Neither of them had faltered. Both their expressions were set.

"Go Callum." Lena said firmly. "We'll be fine. Freya will protect us."

Aaron nodded. "If you hurry you might just catch him."

Callum took Kiera by the hand. Their eyes met. Not another word was needed. They both rose slowly into the air.

The three companions on the ground waved them on their way. "Don't worry Callum," Aaron called. "I'll look after your island while you're gone!"

"That's what worries me!" Callum muttered, as with one final wave, they shot into the night sky.

7

The moment had come. There, buried beneath a thick blanket of snow, the Heart called to her. She could already feel the subtle changes in the world around her as she approached. All she had to do was reach out and touch it...

She had survived death and travelled hundreds of miles without food, water or barest idea of what her final task would be, or even who or what she was.

It was all now so clear.

She was unique in the world – born of union between the two great forces of nature. If the earth were the body then magic was the blood; neither could exist without the other. It seemed fitting then that she should be the one to save them all – seemed fitting that she should be the one to breathe life back into the old world and so right the wrongs of the past.

She knew what she must do.

Slowly, serenely, Phae floated to the ground, her bare, naked feet sinking into the soft white snow. She barely registered the cold – her innate power kept her safe from harm.

The earth called to her. She stepped forward. With a flick of her hand the snow that covered the Heart was swept away. It called her; it beckoned her to approach.

Tentatively, Phae reached forward and began her final task.

* * *

Death landed with a clump. Creatures of the forest scattered in its wake. It was almost as if the forest itself were alive to the intrusion. *Death* snorted angrily as Varrus dismounted. The voice of the star-god thundered inside his head.

"Quickly my servant – the time fast approaches. You must slay the child before my awakening."

Varrus nodded and drew his sacred blade. He did not need reminding of the importance of the task before him. Though he was yet a few hundred yards from the girl's position, he could taste her scent on the cold winter air. "Come girl, your fate awaits you."

Varrus picked up his pace, stumbling over tree roots as he advanced towards the Heart. Even his dark master had failed to foresee the girl's role in the plan's undoing.

A familiar voice echoed through the forest. Familiar, yet somehow different.

"I'm watching you Varrus. The world is shifting. Already you're too late."

Varrus looked about him, aghast. "What? Where are you?"

"I've changed Varrus – I've grown. I'm not the little girl I once was."

Varrus was shaken. The weight of his final task was heavy on his mind. He could feel the star-god's presence begin to grow inside him.

"It begins," the voice of the forest said. "He's coming."

"What? Who, your father? He won't defeat me!"

"Not my father Varrus – the evil one: the destroyer of worlds."

"I know he's coming I–"

The voice of the forest cut him off as he spoke. "You know far less than you would like to admit," the forest said. "Did you not think to question how Skargyr might escape his prison?"

Varrus faltered. "I don't know, I–" Varrus paused. "Anyway, who are you to question me, *girl!*"

"Oh Varrus, Varrus, you just don't understand, do you? The key was never me, or even my father: the key was *you*. Or should I say, *the door.*"

"The door?" Varrus began to tremble. Inside his head, the presence of the star-god continued to grow.

Meanwhile the voice of the forest – the voice of she whom he had once abused for his own ends – was calm and commanding.

"The door Varrus, is you. You are the gateway through which the star-god will attempt to make his escape. For eons the star-god has been imprisoned in the heart of our star – a blazing anathema to the darkness on which he feeds. The sun is his prison and the earth his warden. Magic is the key." Varrus dropped his sword and fell to his knees. The snow was cold beneath his outstretched hands. Slowly, the events since his rebirth were starting to make sense.

"It's over Varrus, you've lost. Your fate is now decided."

For the first time in centuries, tears started to roll down the dark mage's eyes.

"Your tears won't help you Varrus. You decided your own fate and so nearly brought about the destruction of the world. You were only ever a pawn – but a pawn by your own free choice."

Just then the throbbing pain in Varrus' head started to increase. His whole body started to shake.

"So, it begins," the voice of the forest said, as with these words, Varrus' world went blank.

* * *

Though they travelled far faster than either of them had ever travelled before, still they were not fast enough. Callum winced as a wave of energy shot through the magical plain. A tear formed in the corner of his eye. He squeezed Kiera's hand tightly as their eyes met.

"I love you," he said. "I've only ever tried to do my best for you – for Phae, for everyone."

She raised her hand to his cheek and wiped away the tear that ran down his face.

"Callum, I love you with all my heart and more besides. You couldn't have done any more. None of this has been your fault. As ever it seems we are victims of our unique position."

"Are we too late?"

"I hope not. What do your instincts tell you?"

"Something's happening," he replied. "The world is changing."

They flew now, over the Great Forest towards which Lena had guided them. Callum could sense the path Varrus had made through the sky.

"Do you know where we're going?" Kiera asked.

Callum nodded as he took them lower, skimming barely a few yards above the trees.

"I sense him. He's here."

* * *

Phae opened her eyes to find herself standing alone atop a cold stony precipice floating adrift in the dark desolate void. The realm she had entered was a mirror of the star-god's psyche – a sort of "in between" where she knew their final confrontation would take place. Though there was no obvious sign of life she knew that somewhere amidst the darkness the evil one prepared for his final act. On this one rocky outcrop would be decided the fate of the world. For better or for worse she held the fate of everything dearest to her in her small, fragile hands.

She inhaled deeply and felt the warmth of her new powers surge inside her.

At that moment, something started to stir. Though she could not see it at first, a world was forming around her. From her rocky outcrop a bleak, barren plain surged into existence and stretched out as far as her eyes could see. She looked to the heavens as high above her stars burst into being and clouds swirled into life.

Another moment later and the star-god's voice rumbled across his newly-formed domain.

"TREMBLE MORTAL AND KNOW THAT I AM YOUR GOD!"

Phae watched silently as the plain before her started to split. A rent opened in the earth and from the depths of the abyss the star-god emerged. Instinctively, she took a step back. Of all the forms she expected the destroyer of worlds to take she did not expect... a *dragon*.

The great beast surged into the air.

"So, we meet at last."

The dragon turned and swooped towards her. Flame shot from its nostrils.

The flame washed over her harmlessly. Phae was unimpressed. "You will have to try harder than that," she said.

The star-god's powerful voice bellowed from the dragon's lips. "WORLDS HAVE FALLEN AT MY COMMAND AND YET YOU SEEK TO CHALLENGE ME?!"

Phae took a deep breath and sighed. "I don't seek to *challenge* you," she said calmly, "I seek to destroy you completely."

The star-god snorted. "Men and women far greater than you have tried to destroy me but have never succeeded. Beings from across the void have hunted me and sought to bring me to ruin but have failed and suffered endless torment at my hand. What makes you think *you* can stop me?"

Phae stifled a laugh. The more Skargyr threatened her, the more time she bought to complete her task. Though the ancient star-god did not realise it, time was fast running out.

Instead of offering a response to Skargyr's taunts, she stood calm and unmoving, staring straight into the black dragon's eyes. She smiled, for she knew the star-god had lost.

The dragon shot another gout of flame towards her but again she let the searing flames wash over her. The star-god couldn't harm her – she knew this now. For eons Skargyr had conserved energy for this one moment, and now he had little power left to stop her closing the rift and sealing his fate. Even as he fought for freedom, magic was returning to the old world, and soon it would be too much for even one so powerful as he to resist.

Though outwardly she took the form of a small, fragile young girl, she was a girl no longer. She was his destroyer – his antithesis, the saviour of worlds – and he had lost.

The star-god roared. Intense bale-fire erupted from the ground. The stars above burned ferociously as Skargyr realised his impending doom.

"Your anger won't save you," Phae said with remarkable calmness. "Already you are too late. You are trapped between realities and the doors have closed. Your end will soon come."

She watched as all around her the world of the star-god's making started to rip apart. She almost felt sorry for the black dragon as it flew around desperately trying to escape its fate. But then she remembered all the pain, and all the death and destruction the star-god had caused. Skargyr was a blight upon the universe, and she had brought about his end.

She held out her hand towards him as he swooped towards her. A pillar of light shot from her palm. The light engulfed the beast and held it in the air, scorching its dark flesh. The beast tried to resist but she was too strong. She had the strength of a whole world at her disposal.

With a final glance, she squeezed her hand into a fist, and in that moment Skargyr, destroyer of worlds, was no more.

She sighed, her energy spent. She barely had the power left to return to the mortal realm, but before she rested there was just one last thing she had to do.

* * *

Callum started.

Kiera looked at her husband, concern etched upon her face. "What is it?" she asked, "Are we really too late?"

Callum frowned. Something was happening, but he wasn't quite sure what. A strange tingling feeling ran through his fingers.

"Callum?"

He looked at his wife as in that moment he realised what the feeling meant.

He gasped. "We... we're saved," he said at last. "Magic returns to the old world!"

Kiera stared at him with wide eyes. She didn't know what to think. But then she felt it too – as if a giant weight had been lifted from her shoulders.

"But how?" she asked, "What happened? I thought we were too late?"

Just then a voice familiar to them both echoed through the forest. "You were never too late," it said. "You did all you could."

Kiera shot her husband a look. "Phae?" she stammered.

"Yes mother, it is I… or at least a part of me. I am much changed since we last met."

Callum could barely muster a word. He sank to his knees but Kiera caught him and held him in her arms. A tear formed in the corner of his eye. "I… We thought we'd lost you."

"I was never lost father; I was merely called to another task."

"But where are you? What happened?"

The forest stirred. It almost sounded like a sigh. A trail of light illuminated the path before them. "Come, see for yourself."

Tentatively, the two parents walked hand-in-hand through the forest, following the strange trail until at last they came across a small clearing. There, amidst the snow, a crystalline figure lay, naked, but at peace.

They recognised their daughter at once. "Phae!" They both dashed forward. "What's become of you?"

"I am no longer the little girl you remember," the voice of the forest said. "I am as one with the earth now – at one with magic. I am… at peace.

"When the dark mage sent me to my doom the earth bore me down into its core and I joined with it. I was born for this moment – to save the world from darkness and stand as its guardian to the end of days."

"Varrus… Varrus is gone?" Callum trembled.

"Varrus is no more, and his dark master has at last been sent to oblivion. Though I am now weak from my tasks the old world is safe from harm and its people can at last rebuild."

Callum drew a deep breath. Beside him Kiera unmoving. It was all too much for both of them.

"Do not mourn for me mother, father, I am at peace now. I will always be here, I will always watch over you." The voice started to fade.

"Will we ever see you again?"

"Who knows what the future holds," the voice of the forest – the voice of their daughter – replied. "Farewell mother, father. I love you both dearly."

With that the voice faded completely. Callum and Kiera stared at each other in disbelief. Neither knew what to say. Callum reached down and stroked the forehead of the crystalline figure that lay so serenely in the snow. A tear landed on his daughter's lips. "I'm sorry Phae. I'm so sorry."

Kiera put her arm around him and he rose to his feet.

In that small snow-covered clearing, hidden beneath the trees, Callum and Kiera wept. They wept for those they had lost – for the pain that had inflicted them both and brought the world so close to its doom. Most of all they wept for their darling Phae, a little girl no more.

As they stood silently comforting each other in the cold, Callum was sure he could just make out the faint sound of three words rustling through the trees.

"I love you."

Epilogue

It was over – the demons were gone. An eerie silence fell upon the city. No one knew what to do. Some of the survivors broke down and wept while others embraced companions, or offered up a silent prayer for the departed.

At some point during the battle he had lost sight of Lukas and they'd been separated. Though his mind was clouded he was sure he remembered seeing his friend wade into the thickest fighting, throwing himself mercilessly at the demon creatures during what they felt would surely be their final moments on the earth.

Suddenly Edwin's eyes widened. As he started to sift through his memories, one image in particular stuck in his mind.

Lukas had fallen!

Edwin's heart started to race. He searched round desperately but couldn't recognise his friend's face amidst the countless bodies that filled the city streets. Just then a faint voice reached his ears.

"Edwin."

Edwin looked round, anxiously scanning the bodies that lay on the floor. There amidst a pile of demon corpses he spotted his friend, his face bloodied and beaten.

Edwin rushed to his side. "Lukas!"

Lukas coughed violently. His voice was barely a whisper. "Well, it was fun while it lasted eh? Guess you might have to wait a little longer for that drink I owe you."

Edwin's face was pained. Tears started to stream down his face. "No Lukas, don't leave me!" he sobbed. "We'll get you out of here. There's bound to be a healer around here somewhere – this is the Magical Isle after all!"

Lukas shook his head sadly. He coughed again. Blood pooled around his lips. "Look after Ma won't you."

In that moment, Lukas died.

Edwin was speechless. He looked to the sky and howled his grief to the heavens. Without Lukas, he was nothing. He had no one. His life was over.

Just then, a firm hand rested on his shoulder. Edwin turned to see Captain Bridgemore standing beside him, his expression grim. "I'm sorry son – I tried my best I really did. I only wish I could have saved you all…"

Edwin gulped. He didn't know what to say.

They stood in silence for a few minutes.

Eventually, Edwin spoke. "Was it worth it sir? Was it really worth it?"

"I hope so."

"But how will I go on?"

The Captain sighed as he considered his words. "We go on like we always go on son; one day at a time."

* * *

High atop the Wizards' Citadel, Lena surveyed the destruction that had befallen their beloved city. Beside her, Aaron stood, her hand clasped tightly in his own. Unusually, he was lost for words.

Something had happened: something big. She looked to the heavens as far in the distance the first rays of dawn – true dawn – shot over the horizon. The black cloud was no more. Light returned once more to the old world.

The demons had been vanquished and Varrus was gone. All that remained now was to bury their dead and start the long process of rebuilding their lives. She drew in a deep breath and sighed. Aaron put his arm around her.

At that moment she knew everything would be alright.

Aaron shifted as he searched inside his pocket. As he found what he was looking for he clasped a cold metal object into her hand. She gasped as she opened her palm and saw the ring. "I know this probably isn't the best time," he said, "but the Seer said I should save it until we knew we were saved."

Lena was speechless. She'd never seen a ring so beautiful. Her eyes lit up and she flung her arms around him. Their lips met. "Aaron, it's beautiful... I never for a moment expected–" Words failed her as she began to sob. "I love you so much. I've been dreaming about this day for so long I–"

Aaron hugged her tightly as she rested her head on his shoulder. They stood in happy silence, staring out into the horizon. Dawn had come at last.

Just then, Aaron started. Lena looked up at him. He returned her gaze, and then looked back towards the horizon.

"I... I can see!"

THE END

ABOUT THE AUTHOR

Born in deepest darkest Thanet, M.J. Ryder now lives and works in Lancaster (UK) where he is reading for a PhD in English Literature. His website is www.mjryder.net.

34998377R00106

Printed in Poland
by Amazon Fulfillment
Poland Sp. z o.o., Wrocław